In the End

Kellee Kranendonk

Howling Wolf Press

ABOUT THE AUTHOR

Kellee Kranendonk has spent a lifetime writing. According to her late grandfather she was born with pen in one hand; paper in the other. She's certain these days he would claim she was born clutching a laptop.

She's had over a hundred published short stories, poems and articles for both children and adults. A few of her short pieces were to appear in a school project, but the project was cancelled before that could happen. For nine years, Kellee was the editor of an online magazine for young adults. She lives in New Brunswick, Canada with her husband, two of her three children, a sassy dog and two cockatiels.

Acknowledgements

To my husband and children who put up with me, my crazy ideas and long writing hours.

To Howling Wolf for taking a chance on this wild ride.

To Ellen Holder, my editor, for her patience and encouragement.

And to anyone else who may have helped me along the way. You know who you are. My gratitude and thanks to you all.

Contents

Prologue

Moonlight spilled in through a small rectangular window on one side of a nearly empty room. To the left of the window, an ivory pedestal sink gleamed in the semidarkness. On the right, an open cupboard filled with jars and bottles lined the wall, various phases of the moon carved into its vertical boards.

The gray, concrete floor bore a red painted symbol––an unbroken circle with a jagged line through its middle, a solid white orb to the right of the slash.

In the beam of moonlight, a white-robed figure sat cross-legged inside the circle opposite the orb, a hood obscuring the face. A cup of tea and a plate of small cakes sat near its right side. The rich fragrance of cinnamon and vanilla lingered in the still air.

"Bring them," it called in a voice more masculine than feminine.

A door opposite the window opened, and six robed figures entered. Three wore white with hoods hiding their faces. One of them had a small bulge beneath the accompanying belt.

Three wore hoodless red robes. The robes of the guilty. First came a tall, slender man with close-cropped blond hair and a short woman with curly red hair. Behind them came a second woman, slightly taller than the first, dark hair streaming over her shoulders. Her abdomen also swelled beneath her wrap. Finally, the last hooded one.

These two couples stood outside the circle before the lone figure. Except for the blond man, tears streaked all their faces. The other couple in white parted and went to either side of the seated figure.

"Three stand before us guilty," intoned one of the white-robed figures, its voice also more masculine than feminine. "Do you admit your sin here before our great leader, Vainquir, son of the Moon Mother?"

"We do," uttered three voices as one, meek and wavering.

Vainquir rose, stepped toward them. He placed his hand on the shoulder of the last of the four. "Koon, you alone are innocent in this. You may choose to leave, or you can stay and take the punishment with those who betrayed you."

Koon looked to the pregnant woman. She lowered her eyes from his gaze. "You may leave me if you choose," she whispered toward the floor.

He hesitated then turned to Vainquir, wiped away tears and asked, "May I speak, Moon Master?"

Vainquir replied with a single, deep nod.

Koon turned back to the woman, took her hands in his own. He cleared his throat. "We both joined this movement of our own accord." He looked at the small group, including the two in white. "We all did. We accepted all the rules set out for us." More tears slid down his cheeks. "I don't know the reason why, but I still love you, Myst. I choose to stay by your side."

The woman swiped her hand across her eyes as she struggled to maintain her emotions.

"That was beautiful, Koon," said Vainquir. "You alone may join me within the circle."

Koon obeyed.

Vainquir faced the three still before him. "Nylo. Morgana. Myst." Blond, redhead and brunette. The moon washed over all of them. Vainquir removed his hood, never taking his eyes from them. Long hair, silvery in the light, hung over his shoulders. A small red mark on his face glowed faintly, mirroring that of the painting on the floor. He faced the redhead, Morgana. "Your Moon sister's sin is not yours, and you have been betrayed by your bonded one also. But you are also guilty of keeping your own secret."

She gave him a wide-eyed look. Terror. Surprise.

Nylo glanced from Morgana to Vainquir, who continued to speak. "You are the father of her only child. But you told no one of this child."

"Ter . . . Nylo!" cried Morgana.

For the first time, emotion crossed Nylo's face. Shame, sadness. "We were so young," he admitted.

Myst nodded as if she understood. Koon murmured to himself. Vainquir continued. "This child was hidden from me, therefore hidden also from the Moon Mother. Did I not require of you no secrets?"

Head hanging, Morgana nodded against her chest. Nylo stood sentry-like, his jaw muscles throbbing. Myst's eyes widened as if in fear.

Koon wiped a hand over his face, as though trying to pull his emotions out through his pores.

"Will you accept the punishment for your sin against your Moon Mother?"

Again, the nod. A sniff and clearing of throats.

"Very well. Morgana, please join Koon."

She obeyed.

"And now the two of you." He placed a hand on Nylo's shoulder, and one on Myst's. "The power of the Mother is to make us stronger. It is not to be misused."

The two other white robed figures took off their hoods. One had the same silvery hair as their leader, and a glowing mark on its neck; it was impossible to assign a gender. But the other was clearly female, particularly with her bump. A single lock of white lay among her short cropped black tresses. They turned their faces to the light of the moon and began to chant as Vainquir continued his discourse.

"The circle in which I stand represents our unbroken family and the trust we have among us. The bent chevron in the middle represents the power cast down to us by the Moon Mother. The orb to the right, Mother Herself." He turned away from them and joined the chant. "Mother Moon, disobedience has infiltrated our family. Please send down your sign."

A shimmering iridescent mist rose from the circle, bringing the scent of fresh cold, though the temperature of the room did not change.

Lustrous, hazy fingers slid along the cloth of Vainquir's robe. He turned back to Nylo and Myst, placed his hand on her belly. "This is an unsanctioned child, created by two unbonded to each other." He shook his head. "More secrets. But the Mother reveals all to me."

Glistening tendrils rose higher, twisting around the unbonded pair.

"Mother," cried Vainquir as the chanting grew louder. The words were no longer that of any recognizable earthly language. "Please forgive me for not knowing that which you know. Cast your punishment down on those who are deserving."

The chanting stopped. The vapour swirled in a great glittering tornado, the smell of cold, and sour vanilla, invading nostrils. Suddenly thunder crashed. Myst and Morgana cried out then clung to the men at their sides as it echoed throughout the room. With a final roar, the tornado broke open, scattering opalescent dust in a blinding cloud.

Just as quick, it was gone, leaving a death of silence in its wake.

"Moon Master, look!" The silver-haired chanting one brushed soft locks aside to get a better look. One finger pointed at the floor.

The symbolic circle was now broken, void of the joining line in the upper right arc. The chevron in the middle remained the same as did the orb, though the symbol was no longer white. An innocent moon now tainted red.

"Hmmm, yes," said Vainquir thoughtfully. "The circle has been broken." He now addressed the group of four. "Because of *your* sin." His voice took on a monotone. "The power you once received from the Moon Mother is no longer yours, but that of your future. You will know the power by the mark. The chosen ones will have the power to change the future and the past. If they are strong, they can amend the mistakes of the parents."

With one hand on her belly, Myst gazed at Nylo. He gave his head a barely perceptible shake.

"And now all of you, save Koon, must give back what you took from the Moon Mother. Everyone, please step into the circle."

Those in white robes pulled their hoods back over their heads. They first rolled up the right sleeve of Nylo's robe, and then the left sleeves of both women.

"You have seen this done before," Vainquir warned them. "You know the punishment ceremony."

In the silence, except for Koon's sniffles, each of the three held their arms slanted down toward the centre of the circle. Vainquir drew a knife from within his robe. On each of the outstretched arms, he deliberately, delicately ran the silver blade over each one, creating a small incision. A single bloody rivulet ran down each arm, the blood dripping off the end of fingertips and dropping to the floor.

The two in white robes now brought three small yellow cakes and held the pieces beneath the dripping blood.

"Let the Moon's power bind your futures," they both shouted, as if it were a battle cry.

A single bolt of lightning flashed outside the window. Each arm was now cleared of its blemish, as if the skin had never been broken. Bloodied cakes were offered to the sinners.

Vainquir smiled. "You must now eat. Unclean cakes for the unclean."

Trembling fingers took the chunks, gingerly held them to grimacing mouths.

"Bring the boy-child, Thoth," demanded Vainquir when each piece had been forced down each throat.

"No!" cried Myst, wide eyes silently begging Nylo to do something. He bit his lip and gave her another slight shake of his head.

A third hooded figure came through the door carrying a toddler and held him out to Myst. She took the child and examined him. Then, holding a tiny arm in her hand, she cried out, "No! What have you done?"

Startled, the child jumped and began to cry. Myst pulled the little one's head down to her shoulder, her hand caressing his tiny blond curls. The toddler relaxed, wrapping a chubby arm around the woman's neck.

"Your punishment is complete," declared Vainquir. "This child, originally sanctioned by the Moon Mother, also bears your punishment."

Koon sniffed, pinching the bridge of his nose between his thumb and forefinger, looking sadly at the child. A deadly glance to Nylo, then softening again for mother and babe.

"Go now," continued Vainquir, "and follow the path Moon Mother has set before you. Leave this place and live your lives outside the circle. In time the circle will become whole once more."

Sixteen years later

Téa reached out a hand to slap at the alarm that blared at her, accidentally knocking over a pop can she'd brought into her room last night.

The rising sun cast an orangey glow into her room. As she yawned and stretched, she listened for the shouts that usually came from other parts of the house. But there was only silence.

No, not quite. She heard the thump of footfalls, the clink of coffee mugs, the hum of the washing machine.

She sat up and rubbed her eyes, then reached for the can that had fallen to the floor. With another yawn, she began to flip the tab back and forth to break it off. There were recycle bins at school, but they required students to snap off the tabs for an ongoing collection for the purchase of a wheelchair.

Sleep still fogged her brain until a sudden resounding blow made her jump. Most likely her father slapping the kitchen table or the wall as he often did when he thought her mother wasn't listening to him.

"Morgan, listen to me!"

And there it began.

Her mother's name wasn't even Morgan, but sometimes her father called her that. "Just a silly nickname," they told her when she asked about it. At least they hadn't screamed at her.

As sleep fog lifted, she registered pain and looked down to see a small red bead popping out where the metal had sliced across her finger when she jumped. "No," she moaned, dropping the can. She wasn't ready for this first thing in the morning.

Two years ago, when she'd been fourteen, she'd nicked herself shaving her legs. Something she'd done before but had never experienced *the vision*. Thinking it was a dream, or a bizarre one-off, she'd cut herself purposely. Except this time, she'd done it across the strange birthmark she had on her left arm, inside her elbow: a red circle, broken by a jagged slash through the centre, and a red dot to the right of the line.

It had been the same and was always the same when she bled. Thankfully her own menstrual cycle had no effect. She'd sat in her room, too frightened to move, knowing no one would believe her if she told them.

She did ask her parents about the birthmark, that looked more like an odd-coloured tattoo to her. As usual, they yelled at her, making her think she was crazy for even considering that it might be anything but a port-wine stain, as her mother called it.

She tried to avoid sharp things, but sometimes, like now, there were accidents. Closing her eyes, she let herself flow with it.

The figure stood with his back to her. Vague grey, foggy shapes stood to either side of him. Most everything else was blackness. A twinkle of moonlight filtered in from somewhere above them and glinted off something white. Something porcelain, she always thought.

The air smelled cold, and somewhere someone was humming. As she swooped in behind him, he turned and looked right through her. But, with his face a kaleidoscope of colours and shapes that kept changing, she didn't know how she knew he was looking through her. Somehow, she just did.

Unable to stop herself, she reached out to him, knowing that she should have been frightened. Instead, she felt some kind of connection to him, but what that link was, she couldn't fathom. Her father? A teacher? A friend?

Like always, as soon as the thought entered her head, the kaleidoscopic effect of his face drained away and swirled over her, leaving him with an empty black maw in its place.

The columns whisked him away in a grey swirl, his kaleidoscope now blinking and swirling on her arm.

At first, she'd hoped it would go on longer, show her who the male was (she was certain the figure was masculine) and if or how they were connected. But it never did. Was he even someone she could trust, or was he some kind of warning?

Chapter One–Leif and Tea

Leif Noble thumbed a message into the Messenger window, letting himself sway from side to side in the passenger seat, as his friend Stuart navigated turns on the way to school.

"Nine minutes," shouted Dave from the back of Stuart's eight-year-old Honda.

"Just a couple more blocks to go," Stuart assured him.

Leif looked up as they zoomed through a green light at the intersection of Regency and City View streets. Apartment complexes and office buildings slid past behind blurred lines of elm trees, broken only by paved driveways and parking lots. "We'll get there with time to spare," Leif put in.

"Sure, as long as the last light's green." Dave referred to the last traffic light they'd have to stop at before turning into the school's driveway.

Full speed ahead, then Stuart leaned left as he turned and squealed into the student parking lot. Leif shoved his phone into his backpack as they barrelled out of the car and rushed to the front door.

Sitting on the front steps, Leif's younger brother, Jeremy, talked to some girl. What was her name? Tina? "Hey, get your ass to class before you're late!" The words were out before he even knew he was going to say them.

They both looked up at him. "Says the man who's always late. Why do you even care?" said Jeremy, rolling his eyes. "Besides, we've got lots of time. The bell hasn't even rung yet."

"Whatever." Leif looked at Tina, then hurried to catch up to his friends.

"So, why *do* you care if he's late?" asked Stuart.

"Yeah," said Dave. "What's the deal?"

"Just doing big brother duty." Leif shrugged. He didn't really care. What Jeremy did was his own business. But there was something about that girl. Is that why he'd said what he did? He couldn't explain it if he'd wanted to. "Gimme a break!"

The guys nodded, accepting the explanation he gave. Then Stuart asked, "You two study for this morning's history test?"

The question went unanswered as Leif spotted the tall, blond and beautiful Kim. Or maybe it was Kate or Kelli. Whatever it was, he was determined to get her cell number before his buddies did. She had a boyfriend on the hockey team, but rumour was they were breaking up, and Leif wanted to be first in line to date her next. "Hey, think she'll go out with me?"

"Sure," said Stuart. "Why not? All the rest of them hang off you like you're some Norse god or something."

Leif puffed out his chest as the bell rang. "I am, and don't you forget it."

Stuart rolled his eyes, and Dave cracked up. But was it because he genuinely found Leif's statement funny, or because he thought his friend was an idiot and was going to try to get her number first?

Kim/Kate/Kelli turned to them as they walked past. Looking at Leif with knockout blue eyes, perfectly lined with thick black eyeliner and a soft blue shadow, she winked. "Hi!"

Leif stopped, but Stuart grabbed his arm. "Not now, lover boy. You get one more tardy and you'll be suspended."

"Yeah," mocked Dave, pushing him aside. "Big brother duty, remember? Set a good example." He started to speak to the girl, but she ignored him and waved her fingers at Leif. Dave threw his arms up, his reaction matching the disbelief on his face.

Leif smiled at her and yanked his arm out of Stuart's grasp. "Okay, fine! I'm good!"

Although he didn't much care about being suspended, he knew his parents would. Despite being well off, they'd expect him to serve his suspension the same as any other kid in school. He liked to think their money could buy whatever he wanted, but the truth was the wealth didn't make his parents happy. They appeared content and warm outside their home, but Leif saw their reality, could feel their chill, distant attitude to one another. Jeremy never seemed to notice. Or if he did, he never said anything.

"Earth to Leif! You in there, buddy?"

Thoughts interrupted, Leif looked around. Dave was gone, and Stuart was pointing to a doorway. A classroom doorway.

"This is us. First period, remember? What were you thinking about?"

"Girls. Cars. Girls in cars. Pizza!" He followed Stuart into the class as the two of them chuckled at his little joke.

###

Téa Smith sat on the front steps of the school, watching the other kids straggle in. Coloured leaves from the few trees around the school swirled around the parking lot like dervishes in the cool autumn wind. The early morning sun helped to brighten her mood.

She'd left home early, as she always did, just to get away from the nagging.

"Téa, find my blazer!"

"Téa, can you make the coffee?"

Téa this and Téa that. As if she didn't have to get ready to leave the house as well.

She grabbed a donut––there were always donuts––and her Tim's travel mug. Then she stopped for a double-double at the Tim Horton's Coffee Shop across the street.

As the other students arrived via bus, car, or walking as Téa had, she noticed one boy standing alone. Watching her. Gate Williams. The quiet type, he was in one of her classes.

What kind of parents named their child Gate? she wondered. Were his parents naggy like hers? Was he expected to wait on them too? How many of these kids had moms that baked cookies and took them shopping? Her aunt Darla took her, more often than not.

"I bet Gate's mom doesn't," she muttered. "Just like mine." But, of course, just because someone gave their kid an odd name didn't make them a bad parent.

She waved at Gate. Looking confused, he looked around. Seeing no one else, he waggled his fingers at her, took a tentative step toward her. Then he spied Jeremy coming toward her and backed off.

"You scared him away," she accused with a chuckle.

"Huh? Who?" He looked around. "Are you talking about Gate?"

"Yeah, but never mind. I'm kidding anyway." She took a swig of her coffee.

Jeremy breathed deep. "Mmm, coffee. Darla?" He knew about Téa's parents; she griped about them often enough. "And I know you were joking."

"Yeah." Responding to his Darla question, she added, "I started walking her dog a few weeks ago and she gives me money."

"Cool."

Handing him her mug, she grabbed her backpack, yanked open a zipper and started rummaging around.

"What are you doing?"

"I have my schedule in here somewhere. I don't get why they don't just send it in an email."

Jeremy groaned. "In little ol' backwards Shearwood? Besides, haven't you got that memorized yet?"

Téa laughed. "Mostly, but I just want to double-check. Have you got everything memorized yet?"

Jeremy was a grade lower than her, but with her mom working for his parents, she and Jeremy had known each other for a long time. Even lived within walking distance of one another but had only begun hanging out a lot this summer.

When he didn't respond, she darted a look at him. Beneath shaggy brown hair his brown eyes peered back at her sheepishly. He lifted the cup and took a long swallow.

"Hey! Don't drink all my coffee!" she said, grinning.

He handed the cup back to her with a wink.

She'd guided him around the school, watching all the girls stare in jealousy. The younger ones thought he was hot, just like the seniors did with his older brother. But how could two brothers look and act so differently? Leif ate up all the attention while Jeremy seemed oblivious to it, apparently preferring his skateboard. Not even *his* skateboard really, but Leif's old one. Jeremy had no qualms about telling her that either. Leif had abandoned it for the car he'd gotten on his sixteenth birthday (which was in the shop for an oil change and a tune-up. Jeremy had told her that too). Most girls giggled and lavished Leif with the attention he desired. Téa was more comfortable with the down-to-earth younger brother.

Téa shook her head, handed the cup back, and resumed her search. Upon finding what she'd sought, she snatched it out. "Got it!" she cried.

"So, what's first?" He took another drink.

"I said don't drink all my coffee!"

"You keep handing me the mug!"

Pulling a face and sticking out her tongue, she snatched it back, then glanced at her schedule as she drained the cup. "History. Yes!"

Jeremy laughed. "You're the only girl I know, the only *student* I know, who gets so excited over history."

Just then a car zipped into the parking lot, and a moment later Leif and his friends rushed up the steps.

"Hey, get your ass to class before you're late!" Leif yelled at him.

They both looked up. Téa sucked in her breath, her fingers starting to clench.

"We've got lots of time," said Jeremy, "the bell hasn't even rung yet."

"Whatever."

"He doesn't care if *he's* late," Jeremy told her, sighing. "And I doubt he studied last night for his test this morning."

Téa shrugged and relaxed. "So? Let him fail. He's gotta learn some-how." That was her parents' philosophy. She almost regretted saying it, but she wasn't sure how she felt about it yet. Sure, they had a point, but a little more guidance once in a while would be nice. "But hey, guess what?"

"I give up."

She giggled, both at his unwillingness to even attempt a guess, and the look of mock frustration on his face.

"In my history class, we have to do projects. Guess what subject I chose!"

Jeremy groaned and dropped his head to his chest. "You didn't?" he said, not meeting her gaze, pretending he wasn't as excited as she was.

"Yeah, I did," she said, giggling harder.

He grinned. "So, you're doing your project on cults?"

She swatted him with the schedule she still held. "Of course!"

Cults were as much a part of history as wars or styles, and they intrigued her. Why did people join them? Why were there so many different ones? Were there any here in Shearwood? Now or historically?

"You're so weird!" Jeremy teased. "But I have an idea. Why don't you come over to my house. We have this colossal library that you could use. There must be some history junk in there."

"History junk?"

He shrugged, looking sheepish again.

"Is your library really colossal?"

"Well, it *is* really big."

"Great! I'll come by after school. Thanks, Jer."

"Not a problem."

The bell rang. As they rose to enter the school, Téa noticed Gate still watching them.

Chapter Two–Marked

Warm afternoon sun shone down on the half-pipe in the backyard inviting Jeremy outside. He grabbed his skateboard and helmet then started out. Just as his hand met the doorknob, Leif came into the kitchen.

"Where you off to? I thought your girlfriend was coming over to use the library."

"She's not my girlfriend," insisted Jeremy.

"But ya know," started Leif, "she is kinda pretty. Curvy but not chunky. No glasses, not a geek. And you are spending a lot more time with her. What's her name? Toni?"

"Just stay away from her, lover boy!"

Leif could charm an Inuit girl in Iqaluit into buying snow with his good looks, fashionable clothes, and the trendy fads he was always spending money on. Did he do it to make the girls like him? Would they still, wondered Jeremy, if he didn't have money? What would Leif do then?

Their grandmother always said they were "as different as night and day." Most fads didn't have any attraction for Jeremy, and as long as his clothes were neat and clean, he considered them in fashion.

Leif held up his hands. "Hey, she's the daughter of Mom's secretary. That's your style, not mine."

"What exactly is your style?" asked Jeremy, then immediately regretted it. "Never mind, I already know." He hurried out to the yard. He was well aware of Leif's "style" in girls. The kind who were impressed by his money, car, and gadgets. Téa called them "high maintenance girls" and "fake as a threenie." He had no idea what a threenie was until she explained it was something she'd made up; a three-dollar coin, like a loonie or a twonie. Except those were actual coins. "Made up," she'd told him, "just like those girls' faces."

Jeremy didn't think his parents acted that way––they often donated money to charities and other causes they saw fitting––so what had happened to Leif?

Of course, he had no answer. He put his helmet on, then realized he'd forgotten his elbow and knee pads. For a moment he stood there just looking at the half-pipe in his backyard, debating on the pros and cons of going back to the house to get them. Was Leif still in the kitchen? If he was, Jeremy didn't want to hear him yang on about how he should be able to win Téa over with his money.

Téa liked *him*, not his money. But only as a friend. While Leif and his buddies were into the latest gaming systems and pulling all-nighters with girls online, Jeremy and Téa had the most fun doing things that didn't cost anything––like skateboarding, poking around down by the river, or hiking in the woods.

Deciding to take his chances without the pads, he set his board down at the top of the pipe. Just as he slid over the edge, he saw Téa walk up the paved driveway. Distracted for a second, he plunged downward and lost his balance. She ran over to him.

"Hey," he wheezed, raising a hand as if to wave at her.

"Are you okay?" She grabbed his hand and yanked him to his feet. "What are you doing?"

"Wiping out, obviously."

She burst out laughing. Then, trying to stifle her apparent mirth at his misfortune, she said, "I'm sorry. Look, you scraped your elbow."

He twisted around, trying to see the back of his arm. "I'll have you know, I'm usually much better than that."

She smiled. "I know. Let's get you cleaned up so you can show me your library instead of face-planting."

She peered into his face.

He backed away. "What are you doing?"

"Just making sure you didn't scrape up that pretty face. You know, the girls might not appreciate that."

He grunted. "My name isn't Leif Noble; it's Jeremy." He pulled off his helmet. "Besides, don't girls like scars?" He grinned. She rolled her eyes. "C'mon inside," he said.

"Oh my god, Jeremy," she breathed when they reached the library. "It really is colossal. This one room is as big as half my house."

Jeremy had never been to her house, so he took her word for it, realizing she was probably exaggerating, and tried to see it from her point of view. He surveyed the room, built inside a turret-like feature of the house. Except the room wasn't round, only its outer walls were. In here the room had a vaulted, twelve-foot ceiling with shelves reaching about ten feet tall on all four walls. Tall, narrow windows tucked in between each shelving unit were meant to resemble arrow loops in castle walls.

At one end of the room was a wheeled library ladder to reach the upper books, and hanging signs proclaimed what each shelf held: autobiographies, the Noble/Tobias (his mother's maiden name) family trees, documentaries, mysteries, fantasy, fiction and sci-fi. In the spaces between shelf and ceiling hung old tapestries. But don't try to hang anything modern on the walls, he thought.

One time Jeremy had tried to pin up a poster (retro Tony Hawk) on his bedroom wall, and his mother had gotten angry. He hadn't understood what the difference was, so now he just tried to pretend the wall hangings weren't there. Four long tables sat in the middle of the room, placed end to end, each with four cushioned chairs, two per side. There were no ceiling lights in here, but instead each table held a lamp. Slashes of sunlight filtered in through the loops. Almost like a cage or jail cell, Jeremy thought.

"They should have mirrors in here," he whispered in Téa's ear.

She jumped at the sound of his voice, but she smiled, understanding his meaning. He knew she, of all people, would. "Yeah, that would be cool."

He walked over to the table and turned on each one of the lamps so she could better see the books and their titles.

"You need to take care of that elbow first. I'll help."

"No, I'm fine." He held it up to show her.

"Jeremy, blood's running down your arm." She looked at him as if she expected him to do or say something.

"What?"

"Nothing, never mind. Where's your bathroom?"

He grabbed a section of his shirt, wiped the arm, then winced when it hurt. "See? I'm fine."

"Okay," she said holding up her hands, palms out. "If you say so." She went to the history section and ran her fingers over the books, twisting her head to read their titles. "Look at these. I want to read them all."

Jeremy gestured to the tables and chairs. "Have a seat and go at it."

Instead of responding, she rose on her tiptoes to reach for something on a higher shelf. Before he could offer to get whatever it was she wanted, a shout came from behind them. "*What* is that?"

Téa whirled around, pulling a book off the shelf accidentally. Jeremy reached out to grab it and noticed the title. *Shearwood: A History*.

With the book in his hands, he glanced at the doorway. Leif stood there, his eyes wide, his mouth agape.

"What's your problem?" demanded Jeremy.

Leif stalked into the room and stopped in front of Téa. He grabbed her left arm.

"Hey," she and Jeremy shouted together. Téa yanked her arm away from Leif.

"What's your problem?" demanded Jeremy again, poking Leif in the chest.

"Don't start what you can't finish, little brother," warned Leif.

"Oh, I'll finish it," said Jeremy, knowing his threat was empty. His father desperately tried to keep the peace between them, and his mother would punish them both without listening to either side.

Leif reached for him, but Téa put her hand on his chest. "Stop it! What are you even talking about?"

Although she stood up to Leif, Jeremy noted her wide eyes, the hand not on his brother curled at her side.

Glaring at Jeremy, Leif grabbed her sleeve and slid it upward on her arm––the way it had been when she reached upward for the book. "That!"

Jeremy gasped. "Téa! You have one too?" In all the time he'd known *her*, he'd never known about *that*. He stared at it, realizing he'd never seen her in a tank or a short-sleeved T-shirt. She always kept it covered. But now, in her excitement, she'd apparently forgotten and let her sleeve slip, exposing it.

There, on her left arm, was the same reddish mark that Leif had on his right arm––a broken circle, split with a jagged line and a solid orb above and to its right.

Téa whirled around to face Jeremy, pulling her arm once again from Leif's grasp and letting her sleeve fall. She held it against her wrist as if it would fly up her arm of its own accord if she didn't.

"Who else has one and why is your brother int––" She broke off. "You have one too?"

"Not me." Jeremy nodded toward Leif, who had yanked up his own sleeve and was holding out his right arm like some kind of offering.

Spinning back to look at the proffered arm, Téa uttered a little cry. "What is it? What does it mean?"

"How should I know?" growled Leif.

Slowly, almost as if someone else were controlling him, Jeremy dropped the Shearwood history book and reached out to place a finger on each arm. He didn't know what he expected to happen, definitely not what did happen, but he couldn't stop himself.

A cold tingle ran through him, as though he were conducting a flow of electricity. But which way was it flowing? What did it mean? Téa shivered. Leif grimaced. So, they both felt something too. "What is it?" he whispered.

They yanked their arms away. "It has to be something," Téa muttered. "It has to *mean* something."

Leif glared at her and Jeremy a moment longer, then turned and stalked out of the room. Once he was gone, the dream-like aura in the room disappeared.

Jeremy picked up the book and handed it to Téa. She took it from him, looking him in the eye, neither of them saying anything. The words, "What just happened?" were on the tip of his tongue, but he refused to speak them. Their fingers touched. Nothing happened. Not even so much as the nervous thrill of brushing the skin of a pretty girl. Was there something wrong with him? With her?

Suddenly her interest in cults didn't seem so boring after all.

Chapter Three—Into the Basement

Téa piled her books neatly into her locker. The final bell had rung a few minutes ago and the halls were nearly empty, but the scents of sweat, deodorant, and the janitor's cleaning supplies still hung lightly in the air. The silence would have been eerie if not for a muted conversation in one of the classrooms.

She'd scanned most of *Shearwood: A History* last night. But there was nothing in it about cults except to say, "Cults may have existed in Shearwood many years ago, but there is little to no evidence to prove it." Whatever "little evidence" was. The book didn't say.

So, she'd gotten up a little earlier this morning to go to the school library and use the computer there. It was so much easier than using the one at home where someone would be looking over her shoulder, monitoring the sites she visited like she was a little kid. And her parents wouldn't let her have data on her phone; they said she was lucky she even *had* a phone. She found plenty about cults, but nothing in particular about Shearwood:

Many cults worshipped the moon, stars and/or the sun. Sometimes they prayed to a deity of some sort. Bloodletting and visions were often the norm in cults. Some even claimed to see faceless people, rainbows, or any number of things in their visions. Almost all cults have a mark, or a symbol that represents their beliefs.

That part caught her attention. Could there have been a cult in Shearwood that used a symbol like the one on her arm and Leif's? She asked her history teacher, and he said he'd heard rumours about a cult in Shearwood, but apparently it hadn't stayed around very long. That was all he knew. However, he said he was excited to see what she could come up with for her project.

Lying in bed last night, she'd come up with a bizarre plan, and no idea where on earth it came from. She was going to sneak down to the school's basement. What she expected to find down there, she had no idea. But, if cults met in secret, why not in the basement of a school? There might be nothing down there, or if there was, it would probably just be old props for plays and extra desks, chairs, and tables.

But she knew that the school had been built many years ago, at one point serving as more than just a school––a meeting hall, a playhouse, and a public gym had been housed there as well. The playhouse and gym were still there, now for school use only. But as the population grew, so did the need for more classrooms, so the meeting hall had been shifted to the basement, opening up space for more classes. So, the real question was: Why were students not allowed down there?

Did people still meet down there? As far as Téa knew, they didn't. Even if they did, what was the big deal about students going there? What was really down there? Could it be more than just school things, or had her imagination kicked into overdrive?

She headed to the cafeteria kitchen where the basement door was located. A strange place, she thought, for a door no one was supposed to use. Students frequented the kitchen since that was where they bought their hot lunches. But, she supposed, this building wasn't always a school, and there probably wasn't any money in the budget to remodel.

With the kitchen staff gone for the day, she stood in the empty, darkened room and stared at the door as if it would magically open.

Her heart hammered and her guts quivered. A quick glance around showed her she was alone, even though she felt like a million eyes were watching her. In the silence, the ticking of the clock above the door sounded like canon fire.

Had a student ever disobeyed and gone down there? Probably, she figured, but what did they find? Were they punished?

Until now, she hadn't even thought about the door being locked. Which it probably was. *Stupid girl, of course it's locked!*

Still, she couldn't resist trying. Tentatively, she put her fingers on the knob. Squeezed.

Pushed.

Pulled.

Of course, nothing happened.

"What are you doing?"

She squealed and whirled around. Gate Williams stood there giving her a funny look.

"Gate! You scared the crap out of me!" She swatted his arm.

"Well, what are you doing?" he insisted, a partial grin on his face.

She didn't respond. If she told him, would he snitch? He looked like a snitch, with his square-framed glasses, his long black hair hanging over his shoulders (he usually wore a ponytail) and metal braces glittering in his mouth. He had on a black Under Armour hoodie and blue jeans. She certainly didn't expect his next move.

"Never mind," he said. "I know where the elevator is. Come on!"

Did he really expect her to trust him enough to go with him? On the other hand, it was Gate. He was harmless, wasn't he?

He realized she wasn't following and turned back. "Are you coming or not?"

Didn't you just consider him a snitch? Téa gawked at him, debating. What did a snitch even look like? Besides, if he told on her he'd get into trouble too. Unless he lied, in which case it would be her word against his. If he tried something a little more physical, she could handle that. But defending herself against his lies––

"You wanna know what's in the basement, don't you?" he asked, breaking into her thoughts. His grin unsettled her. How did he know? But when she asked, he only said, "Why else would you try that door?" He pointed to it, behind her.

"Have you ever been down there?" she asked.

"No, I just know another way to get there. C'mon."

He stood waiting for her. Part of her screamed *run away*, the other part burned with curiosity, a need to know what was hiding in that basement. And in that moment, she was certain something *was* down there. She grinned, then followed him past the cafeteria, down the stairs, and through the hall to the office. A few people were still there working, but none of the workers so much as glanced up at them. It was perfectly normal for students to be there for extracurricular activities, tutoring, or getting extra help in subjects they struggled with.

Gate pushed through a set of double doors that led to the bottom floor via two ramps. Classes were set up down there for disabled students, most of whom were unable to use the stairs. Téa had never even been on that level before.

At the end of another long hallway, a grey door was marked "Janitor." Gate pushed it open and stepped inside. Téa stayed where she was.

"Are you coming?"

She shook her head. Following him had been a bad idea after all. He'd tricked her and just wanted to get her alone in an obscure place.

"Look, the elevator to the basement is in here. You said you wanted to go down there."

Elevator? Had he said that before? Téa couldn't remember now, her emotions swirling within her. She held his gaze, said nothing at first. "Never mind," she muttered and turned to leave.

"Hey, wait! Téa! I'm not going to hurt you or anything like that. I promise."

She turned back. "Elevator, Gate? Seriously? That's really funny. Ha ha! I'm leaving."

"No, wait!" He flipped on the light and pointed to the back of the small room. Faded black spray paint covered a set of elevator doors. White block letters spelled **OUT OF ORDER.** But a little button beside them showed a red arrow pointing down.

Téa glanced up at the overhead fluorescent light fixture. "Maybe you should have led with that."

Gate grinned, the guilt on his face as clear as the words on the elevator. "Yeah, sorry."

"How did you know where to find this anyway? No able-bodied person ever comes down here. And you look pretty able-bodied to me."

"How do you know no able-bodied people come down here?" he asked. "I mean, the teachers––"

"Do the teachers use this elevator?"

Gate studied her, as if wondering whether or not he should let her in on something. Or maybe he was wondering if she'd been coming on to him. Just as she was about to dissuade him, he finally said, "Can you keep a secret?"

"Sure." He had no more reason to trust her than she had to trust him, so she guessed they were even. If his secret turned out to be anything, that is.

He lowered his voice, as if he needed to. "I overheard my mom and dad talking. They were talking about Atlas. He's my uncle."

"Atlas, the janitor?"

Gate nodded.

Atlas wasn't his real name, but the students called him that because one time a student had asked him why he was so quiet and never spoke with anyone. His response had been that he carried the weight of the world on his back. No one knew what that was supposed to mean, but someone had called him Atlas and it stuck. Despite his apparent lack of interest in the students, he seemed to enjoy his job.

"He's your uncle? Okay, so that's not such a big secret."

"No, not that part. My parents were talking about him because that elevator is here in his "office." He hooked his fingers in the air. "Apparently the three of them were part of some cult right here in Shearwood, and it had something to do with the school. I don't know what; I didn't hear everything."

Téa's heart skipped a beat. A cult! Here in Shearwood! Should she show him the mark on her arm? Did he have one as well? She realized he was still talking.

"Hold it. Wait, what?" she cut in.

"What?" he asked.

"What did you say?"

He sighed and rolled his eyes. "I said that's where Mom and Dad met. Mom even dated Roger, I mean Atlas, for a while. I think they left after I was born."

"They left the cult? Why? Didn't they allow kids?"

He shrugged. "Yeah, the cult. And I don't know if they allowed kids. I'm not sure if they actually left then, I just think so. I couldn't very well ask them."

"Is it still around?" She tugged at her sleeve, still debating on whether or not to show him her birthmark.

"No idea. If we can get down into the basement, maybe we can find out." He headed toward the elevator.

Still, Téa remained where she was. That was why he was so eager to get her down here. He had questions that needed answering too, and he wanted a partner in crime. The mark on her arm itched and burned, felt like it was alive. She wanted to scratch it, cut it, to see the faceless person. Was it Gate? Was he connected to her? Is that why he just so happened to show up when he did? Did he somehow know she was going to be there? But what about Leif and his mark?

"Hey, you coming?"

She curled her hands into fists to avoid touching her arm. She took a step. Finally, she could take it no longer. "Gate!"

He startled and his eyes widened. "What? Are you okay?"

Wrapping her right hand around her left elbow, she said, "Do you have any kind of birthmarks?"

"What? No." He frowned, confusion in his voice and in the wrinkles on his forehead.

"Don't you ever dare to tell anyone," she said, "because if you do, I'll--" She lifted her hands, fingers curved into claws. What exactly would she do? Rip out his tongue? She shivered at her own violent thought and dropped her arms to her sides. But her gesture had already been enough.

"Whoa!" His eyes widened even more, and he took a step back, raising his hands in the air. "Jeez, I promise, okay? Just don't hurt me."

Téa paused only a moment to gather herself before holding her arm out and lifting her sleeve. "I won't as long as you don't say anything."

Gate sucked in a heavy breath, then clamped his hand over his mouth. He looked at her, eyes wide behind his glasses. "I knew it!" he burst out.

Then he shook his head and settled back, seeming to recover from letting her in on a much bigger secret, one he wasn't supposed to tell.

"What? Gate, what are you talking about?" Could he really be the one from her vision?

Despite his sudden chill act, his eyes shone with excitement, and he became more animated than usual. Most of his answers in class were monosyllabic, unless forced to say more. Then he usually just sounded bored. "It's just a feeling. You said in class you wanted to do your history project on cults. That was my choice too, even before you said it. There's a connection between us, Téa, and I think it has something to do with this cult. Were *your* parents in it too?"

She recalled him watching her, backing off when Jeremy approached, but not leaving. Was he crazy or was he onto something?

"Can I touch it?"

Remembering the tingle she'd felt when Jeremy had touched her arm and Leif's, she pulled her sleeve down. "No."

"So, were they? Your parents I mean. In the cult?"

"I don't know. I don't think so."

"Yeah, well, it's not likely they'd tell you even if they were."

"Nope!" She knew that was the truth. "Are you sure you don't have a mark like this anywhere on your body?"

"Not anywhere I can see." He pulled off his hoodie revealing a T-shirt beneath. "How about on my back?" He untucked the back of the shirt.

"Wouldn't your parents have told you if you had one?"

He shrugged. "Maybe, maybe not."

Téa understood that too. She lifted the tee higher so she could see his shoulders, lifted his hair to check his neck. "I don't see anything. And I'm not checking anything in this area." She poked a butt cheek.

He pulled his hoodie back on as his face reddened. "Damn! I wonder why you got marked."

"Why I . . . you think it's a cult mark?"

"It's too uniform to be a birthmark. It's a symbol, Téa. I mean it sure looks like one. Unless it's a tattoo."

Téa rubbed her finger over the reddish mark that her parents claimed wasn't a tattoo. She damn well wasn't going to tell Gate about Leif or the visions. At least not yet. He'd get unhinged if she did, regardless of whether it was him in the dream or Leif.

But if it was a cult mark, why didn't Gate have one? Is that why his parents had left the cult? Because they didn't want their baby boy to be tattooed? So many more questions crowded her brain. Her parents, Leif's. Were they all a part of some secret group? Were they still? Did they meet here in the basement? Who else knew about it?

"The elevator must work, right?" he said.

She looked at Gate who was looking at the elevator doors, fixing his clothes.

Before she could point out the obvious warning in white lettering staring him right in the face, he poked the button.

They heard clanking, whirring, thumping. Then the red button turned green.

"Hey, it does! Come on!"

Stranger still, she thought as she followed him, feeling like Alice going down the rabbit hole.

"Why would it be marked out of order if it works?" he asked.

"Yeah, so weird," she muttered. But was it really?

When the elevator stopped, and the doors opened, they found themselves in a long, dank hallway lined with doors. Emergency lights beside each door dimly lit the corridor. At one end were broken stairs.

Before she could ask about them, Gate asked, "Do you smell that?"

"Musty, moldy basement? Yeah, I smell it."

"No, not that." He sniffed. "It's like roasted chicken."

Téa took a breath. "Oh my god, Gate, that's so weird." Monsters wriggled in her gut and ghosts tickled the back of her mind. Goose-flesh rose on her skin, not necessarily because of the dampness. Her adrenalin level rose, pushed her heartbeat faster. She was both creeped out and excited at once.

Sniff, sniff. "It's gone now. Maybe we're imagining things."

"Maybe." Were phantom smells a thing? Téa tried to remember if she'd read about that anywhere, but her mind refused to go there.

Gate started to walk along the hall. "Why aren't there classes down here? These rooms are perfect."

"How should I know?" Téa hadn't meant to snap, but something felt off down here besides her guts. Like they weren't even at the school anymore. "Was this, or *is* this the meeting hall?"

Most of the doors were solid, with no windows. Gate found one with a narrow window and peered into it. "Dark. Can't see anything. But it might have been at one time. I don't think it's used anymore. Doesn't look like it anyway."

"Try the door," said Téa in a voice she couldn't raise above a whisper.

He tried the knob, but it was locked. "Let's try all the doors," he suggested.

After they'd rattled each knob, they found only two were open. The first room was empty. No windows, no furniture, nothing. Even the walls were bare.

But in the second room, there was a bit more. A small, high window let in some natural light. Below and to the right was a pedestal sink, its porcelain chipped and dusty. Téa gasped as a memory flitted through her mind.

"What is it?" asked Gate. "What's wrong?"

"Never mind. It's nothing."

Gate grabbed his phone, turned on the flashlight feature and shone it over the walls. "Look at this!"

Hanging on one wall was an open cupboard stocked with a few jars and bottles, most either lying on their sides or broken. Whatever had been inside had long ago dried up and lost its smell. Moon-shaped figures were carved into the vertical side boards.

Téa stifled another gasp, her heart hammering in her chest.

"Turn on your flashlight," Gate instructed.

She pulled her phone from her back pocket, but when the screen lit up, it showed only 14% in the upper corner. "Not enough battery power."

He didn't respond, just played the light along the floor. Nothing but bare concrete. Suddenly he dropped to kneel on the floor. "Gotta be paint," he muttered.

Looking down at the floor, she saw spatters of red. Had someone spilled paint? Or had the floor actually been painted once? Gate reached out to touch it, then froze. "It's wet!" he cried.

"I'm outta here!"

"Téa, wait!"

She ran out of the room and didn't stop until she was back in the lower hallway of the school in front of the elevator, her finger poised over the red button. If Gate didn't hurry, she was leaving without him.

A second later, the light beam from his phone came out of the room, followed by Gate. Téa jabbed the button.

"It was paint, Téa," he said as he caught up to her and they stepped into the carriage. "It had to be! Blood doesn't stay red--"

"Gate! Everything in that room was dusty, dirty, and broken. There's barely any light down here. How can it be paint? *Wet* paint?"

"Well, how can it be blood?"

"You wanna go back down to check?"

"Maybe."

"Then go by yourself."

The elevator stopped. Gate followed her out, but she was no longer in a mood to deal with him and whatever had just happened. This time when he called to her, she didn't stop. Just kept going until she got outside, paused only to take a deep, cleansing breath, then headed home before Gate could catch up to her.

Chapter Four—Inside the Visions

Téa sat in her Aunt Darla's Ford Escape, waiting for her to finish pumping and paying for gas. Gate hadn't been in class today, but Téa was sure it had nothing to do with yesterday's incident. Her mind kept wanting to go back there. *What was that red stuff on the floor? Why was it wet?* So, she'd put on some music and immersed herself in a book.

Back in the car, Darla asked, "Okay, so supper first? I'm starving. Is McD's okay? Oh, and have you called or texted your mother to let her know?"

She answered Darla's multiple questions, touching her thumb to a fingertip with each response. "Sure. It's fine, and not yet." She dug out her cell.

This little excursion downtown hadn't been planned. Darla had stopped by the school on a whim which, as far as Téa was concerned, was perfect.

Mom Darla picked me up after school. Going shopping. see u L8r

"She's going to have a screaming fit."

"My sister always has a screaming fit about something," Darla replied. "Let me handle her when we get back, okay?"

Téa nodded. Better Darla than her.

Pulling out of the gas station on the corner, which was just down the street from the school, Darla drove down Hill Street. The school was at the top of a hill (uptown). Downtown was a shopping district at the bottom of that hill. Téa often wondered how flat cities distinguished their uptown from downtown.

The restaurant where they ate had a great view of the Commerce River. It ran between Shearwood and Walkerton, often called the Twin Cities.

The buildings in this area sometimes flooded in the spring when the Commerce overflowed its banks, but Téa still loved coming here at all times of the year, both with Darla and Jeremy. She often thought it might be nice to live down here near the river, despite high water levels, rather than up so close to the school. That way she and Jeremy wouldn't have to catch a city bus just to come down here to hang out in Riverside Park, go to the pool, or walk by the river as they had done this summer. She'd still have to take the school bus, but that didn't cost her money. Jeremy had paid her way most of the times they used the city transit, but she hated it even though he couldn't have cared less.

"Look at the sun-diamonds sparkling on the river," Darla said around a mouthful of cheeseburger. "Isn't it gorgeous?"

Téa nodded. The Commerce was definitely that.

"I've always wondered why they call it The Commerce? You probably know, don't you?"

Téa plucked a fry out of its little white bag and pointed it at Darla. "Because commerce is business, like trading, buying, selling. And the people that lived here used to do all their trading and buying via the river." She popped the fry in her mouth.

Darla looked at her niece. "Impressive. So, tell me what Shearwood used to be called. I know it had another name, but I don't know it. For that matter, why Shearwood? Why not River Town or something?"

"It was called Epjilasi. Shearwood is a misspelling of Sherwood."

"Like the place where Robin Hood lived?"

"Yeah, I guess. When the first settlers came over here, they wanted to call it Sherwood Town. It got spelled wrong, then shortened to Sherwood. Or Shearwood."

"How do you know all that stuff?"

"I read."

"So do I," said Darla. "But I can't remember all those facts."

"I can because I think it's fascinating."

"*You're* fascinating. Anybody ever tell you that?"

"No, but Jeremy once said I was amazing."

Darla gave Téa a half-smile, almost like she felt sorry for her. But Téa had stopped feeling sorry for herself long ago. Things were what they were, and she wasn't going to get ahead by pitying herself. Having Jeremy say that about her gave her a warm feeling, and she treasured it. Darla was the first one she told. Darla could appreciate it and not scoff at the compliment. Téa shrugged. "I think he's delusional."

"Listen, kid, don't sell yourself short. You're beautiful, you're smart, and--"

Just then a loud group of boys entered, laughing and bantering with one another. Téa recognized Leif; for once, he didn't have his phone in his hand. When he looked her way, she waved and said hi. He turned away without a word or a gesture.

"Well, that was rude," said Darla as Leif's friends began teasing him. She watched them behave like twelve-year olds. "Is Jeremy like that too?"

"Oh god, no! He's totally different from Leif. Jeremy is so chill. *He* doesn't show off like he's the King of the World."

Darla nodded. "His father is like that too. I mean, I've only met him a few times, but every time he was so quiet and laidback. I've heard that he's the better doctor of the two, as far as bedside manner. Apparently, Elaine is very cold and rigid."

"I've only spoken to them a couple of times too, but they seemed nice."

"Actually, Leif reminds me of your father."

"What? Maybe *you're* delusional." Téa grinned, then giggled.

Darla grinned back with a snort. "I probably am. But as long as I've known Terry, he's always had this way of thinking he's always right and better than most others. That sound like Mr. Noble over there?"

Téa nodded. Yep, that sounded like Leif all right. And her father enjoyed being the centre of attention too. Between her father's attitude and her mother's drinking, she was surprised they managed to hold onto their jobs. She looked at her aunt as a thought occurred to her. Were they only employed because they worked for the Nobles?

"How long have our parents known each other?" she asked. "I mean mine and Leif's. Did the Nobles just hire the Smiths because they're friends?"

Darla nodded. "I think so. They've been friends forever, as far as I can remember."

So that was it. Best friends who overlooked bad habits, covered for their buddies. Téa's mind briefly flashed on her conversation with Gate yesterday. Buddies? Or was it more complicated than that?

#

Téa lived in a remodeled, eighty-year-old, two-story house that her parents had bought just before she was born. It was just outside the area of Shearwood proper known as Hall Town, still within walking distance of the school. Rows of homes along several streets, known as Hall Houses, were built for soldiers coming back from war. Mr. Garnet Hall had sold off a sizeable chunk of his farmland to the government for this purpose.

When Darla finally dropped Téa off at home, the house was quiet. Like normal people lived there instead of a constantly quarrelling couple. Bright white light filled the big living room window, and the smaller kitchen window glowed soft yellow from a night light.

Téa didn't say anything as she got her shopping bag out of the backseat. Darla had bought her a pretty, deep purple bra (with a lot of lace) and loaned her money to buy a pair of jeans that were on sale. She'd have to take Murphy for a few more walks to pay her aunt back.

Before Téa could thank Darla, her mother came running outside, yelling.

"Téa! There you are! I was so worried. Where were you? Why didn't you call? You know you're supposed to call or text to let me know where you are. I didn't know you weren't going to be home, so we ordered out."

All of this in one breath. Téa gripped her bag handles a little tighter, wishing she were invisible. Darla climbed out of the car. "Erla, calm down. She *did* text you. I saw her."

For a moment Erla was still, as if debating what her next move should be. Then she shrieked at her husband. "Terry! Where's my phone? She said she sent me a text. Terry, have you seen my phone?"

Erla ran back into the house, yelling at the top of her lungs.

"Will you be okay?" Darla asked.

Téa shrugged. "I always am."

Darla came around the car to give her a hug. "As usual, call me if you need to."

As Darla got back in her car, Téa nodded, then started into the house. She could hear her mother's voice, fainter now, still screeching about her phone. Téa turned back. "Oh, Aunt Darla?"

"Yes?"

"Um, first, thanks for everything, and second, who's Morgan?" Téa wondered why she'd never thought to ask Darla before.

"I don't know anyone named Morgan. Why?"

"Sometimes Dad calls Mom that."

"Really? Weird."

"Yeah, he says it's some stupid nickname."

Darla laughed. "Oh yeah, like *Captain* Morgan. You know, as in rum."

Then it clicked for Téa. That was it of course. Except that Captain Morgan was a guy, but whatever.

She watched Darla pull away, then went inside. The "Captain" and her father were still arguing, Téa's absence apparently forgotten. Erla directed Terry on how to dial her number so she could find her missing phone. As if dear old Dad didn't know how to use a cell phone. He told his wife as much, beginning with, "Shut up, Erla."

Walking through the living room, still wearing sneakers, Téa stifled a chuckle.

Not only because of her parents' argument, but also because her mother would have had another fit over the shoes if she'd been paying attention.

Down in her bedroom, Téa admired the bra and jeans in the full-length mirror on her closet door––the mirror Darla had bought for her thirteenth birthday.

The jeans fit her perfectly, and the bra was the prettiest one she owned. Before changing into pajamas, she stayed in front of the mirror, trying to see herself through someone else's eyes. How did others see her?

Jeremy called her eyes honey brown. Even a girl in one of her classes had told her she had beautiful eyes. So at least someone thought she was pretty. Hadn't Darla said that today? She tried to recall their conversation at McDonald's, but her memories were tainted by the actions of immature boys. No matter, Darla had said it before. If she was pretty, then why hadn't her parents ever told her?

"Because," she said, leaning forward and looking into her own eyes, long brown hair falling over her shoulders, "they're too busy making a fuss over whether I'm too fat, or the kind of cosmetics and clothes I wear. Because they're too busy fighting each other."

At least she'd done a good job with her eyeliner this morning. That was courtesy of Darla's "secret" makeup lessons. They'd watch YouTube tutorials together, then practice on each other. They weren't really secret. Erla knew, but as long as Téa didn't bring it up, her mother usually just gave her disapproving glares instead of the nth degree about where she'd been.

A smash against a wall made her wince. Obviously, the argument had escalated as usual. She wondered if her mother had even found her phone and the text, but decided she must have, or Erla would have been downstairs demanding that her daughter find it for her.

She used to cry about it––before, during, after. Gradually her tears dried up. She still didn't like it, but no tears or any amount of anger was going to change it, and she was no longer willing to waste emotion on people who didn't return it.

Straightening up, she reached to take the bra off and let her gaze go to her left arm. Leif had a mark, but Gate didn't. Yet his parents were in whatever cult had existed there. And the school basement. So creepy! What had been on the floor, and who had put it there? Obviously, someone else had been down there besides her and Gate. Where had they been hiding? She shivered. They could have been anywhere, watching, listening.

"What's going on," she asked herself as she slid on her pajamas. "And how am I ever going to find out?"

# # #

In the morning, Téa woke to the sound of rain beating against her window. That was all, only rain. Her parents must have been still snoozing. She rolled over and tried to go back to sleep herself, but the image of the mark and what it meant and the stuff in the school basement kept creeping into her thoughts. She tried to focus on the rhythm of the rain gently intruding on the silence of her house, but the eerie memories of her escapade with Gate refused to stay away this time.

Finally, she crawled out of bed and started up the stairs. She could make a cup of coffee and grab a donut or bagel, then go back down to eat in her room. Maybe read or try to figure out what to put in her school project.

Twin snores came from her parents' bedroom. First Mom, then Dad. Or maybe it was the other way around.

Then she remembered the shattered glass from yesterday and went back down to get her sneakers. She didn't feel like dealing with the vision today.

Upstairs, she found jagged shards from a small round vase that had sat in the middle of the coffee table, looking as lonely as she often felt, without flowers to beautify it. Most of it she would vacuum up later when her parents got out of bed, but first she had to pick up the larger pieces. Carefully, so she wouldn't cut herself. As she picked up the last one, her finger slid across a serrated edge. Dammit, why hadn't she thought to wear gloves? To protect her hands the way she protected her feet. Stupid girl!

She ignored the pain that sliced into her as the vision slithered into view.

The figure stood with his back to her. Vague grey, foggy shapes stood to either side of him. Everything else was blackness. She peered at him closely. A twinkle of moonlight filtered in from somewhere above them, bathing the figure entirely in its glow. Blond hair or moonlight-washed black hair? Style was indistinguishable, as the hair looked more like tousled bedhead than anything else. It did seem to have some length to it, though.

The light glinted off the white porcelain sink. The one at the school? She tried to look at the floor, but the vision swooped her in behind him. He turned and looked right at her. That was different. He never looked at her before, always through her, although she wasn't sure how she could tell the difference. She still couldn't see his face, but it had to be Gate. Her assumption felt both right and wrong.

As usual, she reached for him. This time, he reached back. The grey columns moved away, dissipating in the darkness as their fingers touched. The kaleidoscope drained away from his face, leaving the black maw as always. Except now the colours filled up their hands and arms, swirling, blending, becoming a single colour. Blood red.

Pooling where the crooks of their elbows and the marks would be, red colour streamed down their arms like real blood and dripped off their fingertips. The vision didn't stop. Even when Téa tried to pull away. It was impossible to tell where she stopped, and he began. She tried to scream, but no sound came out of her mouth.

A thick mist rose up, shimmering around them both. She looked at his face again, hoping to see Gate. Surely he'd know what to do.

A face began to emerge from the blackness. "You!" he cried.

"Oh my god," she returned. "Let go!"

He tried, she tried, but the mist intensified, formed itself to them and bound them to each other.

# # #

Waking to the steady thrum of rain against metal roofing, Leif groaned and rolled over. So much for hanging out at the track today.

Yesterday he and Stuart had agreed to accompany Dave to the track while he ran practice laps on his motorbike. Leif wasn't into bikes, but there were sure to be girls there. Sadly, Dave's hot sister Mandy wouldn't be there. He was under no delusion that she would've dated a high school student, but she had treated him like an adult, like the ideas and opinions he had might be worth something, not just the whims of a kid.

She died tragically the year before, when she'd accidentally overdosed on drugs. She was only in her first year of college.

Leif took it harder than he let anyone believe, laughing and carrying on despite the ache in his heart. He avoided Dave for as long as he could before Stuart made him get his act together. Now Dave rarely spoke about her, but he told Leif that a guy she hooked up with had given her some kind of drug. The guy had confessed, then disappeared. Today would have been the first day Dave had gone to the track in nearly a year. Mandy had loved bikes too.

Rolling to his back and throwing his arm over his eyes, Leif tried to sleep, but instead of soothing him, the sound of the rain drilled into his ears, giving him a headache. He sat up and pressed his fingers against throbbing temples. Suddenly the mark on his arm turned cold. He shivered as the chill raced through his body. "What's happening?"

His voice sounded faraway. Without a thought, he rose and crossed the room to rummage in his jeans pocket. He watched the movements of his hands through a haze, as if someone else controlled him. Finding the Swiss pocketknife he'd gotten for Christmas a few years ago, he pulled it out. Eighty-three functions, but he only needed one. The mini screen on one side read 7:03. He barely registered how early it was.

Returning to his bed, he held out his arm, hands trembling. He paused, eyes on the mark. It appeared to rise from his skin as pearly red mist. Again, he watched as his hand pressed the tip of the blade into the circle inside his right elbow, his fingers sliding through the haze, a single droplet of blood slipping from the miniscule slice in his skin. No, he didn't want this to happen. Had never wanted it to happen. But he couldn't stop himself . . .

The girl stood with her back to him. Long, dark hair fluttered as though she stood in the wind. But there was something different about her this time. The colours that he usually saw, where were they? She turned to face him, her face ghostly pale. Téa! Had it really been her all along? Why?

She raised her hands. He saw himself reach up and wrap his fingers around her wrist, the colours leaking from his own hands into hers, writhing, becoming blood dripping from . . . where did she end, and he begin?

She screamed, cried out for him to let go.

He tried.

She tried.

Mist, like the stuff from his arm, mixed with the colours and bound them to each other. He looked at her face, hoping it wasn't really her, hoping he would wake up.

But it was her and he couldn't wake up.

Chapter Five—The School

The mist pressed in around them, forcing them together. The thumping that began to echo in Leif's ears was, he realized, not rain but the sound of their hearts pounding out of sync. The beat pulsed harder and faster until suddenly it stopped in a flare of light. The burst ripped them apart.

Leif flew back, away from Téa, but not before he had seen her illuminated in the flash. She no longer had a face. Where it was supposed to be, was nothing but an empty, black hole.

He screamed, only stopping when the punch of metal on flesh and bones drove it out of him. With something solidly behind his back, he drew a shuddering, gasping breath. The mist faded away; his surroundings came into focus.

Two bright orange doors, each one with a stick figure on it, set into a cinderblock wall, told him exactly where he was. But how had he gotten there, at his school? He automatically reached into his pocket for his phone, but it wasn't there.

He heard a gasp beside him and glanced over. Téa sat staring at him with wide eyes, struggling to breathe. At least she had her face back. Leif scrambled to his feet, already knowing he'd find grey lockers behind him. He also knew how to get out of there.

Drawing another deep breath, he rounded the corner beside the orange washroom doors and pushed on the glass and metal exit/entrance doors. They refused to budge. Locked! Of course they are, he thought. It's Saturday. Maybe someone had forgotten to lock a door somewhere, in the gym maybe, or the shop.

He zipped back around the corner and saw Téa on her feet. "Check all the doors, there's gotta be a way out," he demanded, rushing past her and down the hall.

It occurred to him mid-step that locked doors were usually meant to keep people out, not in. But the doors were locked from the outside! How many times had he joked about this place being a prison? It didn't seem so funny now.

"No!" he roared, tearing off again.

In the gym, he shook the metal push-bar across the door. It didn't budge. He slammed the side of his fist against the cold, steel slab, feeling nothing. There were still more doors to check, though. Swallowing the panic that rose inside him, he whirled around, intent on leaving the gym.

Suddenly the size of the room overwhelmed him, its proportions swelling like a growing tsunami. The basketball nets at each end and the bleachers on one side appeared to be made for giants. The school's hockey team logo, "The Shearwood Scorpions," painted on a wall on the other side seemed alive and menacing. Its claws lazily snapped open and closed, its tail hung out from the wall, jabbing like it wanted to sting him. Leif's heart raced, his skin sticky with sweat. He closed his eyes, waiting for a jab that would either kill him or wake him up.

What if he was trapped in here? Would anyone miss or remember him? Kelli/Kim/Kate? Dave and Stuart? Would they miss him or his money? Would everything about him just become a memory, faded and relegated to the farthest corners of everyone's mind?

What about his family?

"No!" he shouted. The sound bounced around the enormous space sounding small and insignificant to his ears. He had to get out of there. But how? Wait until Monday?

"I have to be dreaming, right?" he muttered to himself. Still the sound echoed, hissing through the air. "I just need to wake up." He opened his eyes. The scorpion logo was just that again––a painting on a wall. But he was still at the school.

He headed across the gym, each step sluggish like he was mired in something. Water or muck. No matter how many steps he took, it seemed he wasn't getting anywhere. His legs grew tired, as if he'd run several laps.

"I just need to make it to the door beside the bleachers," he mumbled to himself. That entrance only led to changing rooms, showers, washrooms, and an equipment storage room, but at least it was a goal.

"Hey," he yelled. "Someone wake me up! Jeremy? Dad? Mom? Anyone?" His voice did nothing but echo in the big hollow room.

Step, step, step. Each one a struggle, his legs heavy now, as if weights were strapped to them. He stopped and lowered himself to the floor, stretching out as though he were on his bed. He closed his eyes again, relishing the coolness of the floor against his hot sweaty face. "Wake up," he murmured.

It wasn't a very good dream anyway. No girls, no cars. Nothing like his usual dreams.

The gym spun, or at least felt like it did. He squeezed his eyes tighter until the sensation went away. When he opened his eyes for the second time, he was still at school, but at least the gym had shrunk to its original size.

He stood and lifted his left hand to touch his hair. Curls still gel-stiffened. But what did it matter now?

In the boys' washroom, he splashed cold water on his face, looked at his reflection, tapped the mirror, laid his hand flat against it. Everything seemed real. "But it can't be, right?" he asked his image.

He half expected it to respond. When it didn't, he headed for the cafeteria, down the hall from where *whatever it was* had dumped them.

Téa was nowhere in sight. She had been with him, hadn't she? The one in the vision? Or was that part of the dream? Maybe she was off checking doors or slogging through some other hopped-up-on-steroids room.

Sighing, he dug into his jeans pocket, then remembered that his cell wasn't there. How was that possible? He always had his phone, even in his dreams.

He didn't come up empty-handed though. A golden coin stamped with a loon glittered in his palm. A loonie. One Canadian dollar. Closing his fingers over it, he went to the pop machine, just outside the cafeteria, against a wall behind which was some kind of storage room. He deposited his money and pressed a button. A shiny, wet can rumbled out. He snatched it, popped the tab, and began to chug.

Behind him, someone cleared their throat. Leif nearly choked on the bubbly liquid running down his own throat. Spinning around, he found Téa standing there. So, she really was here with him.

"What?" he snapped, annoyed at being startled.

"Are you going to share?"

He frowned, swallowed, then looked at the red and white pop can in his hand. Back to her. Fog shrouded his brain, and any response he might have been able to give her was lost. She shook her head then walked away. *What's wrong with me?* He raised the cold can and rolled it across his forehead. So cold! Why was he feeling so much if this was just a dream?

He considered calling after her, to ask what she had experienced, or if she'd found an open door. He stopped before the sound of his voice left his throat. If he couldn't get himself out of his own dream, she certainly couldn't.

# # #

A faceless monster appeared in the flash of light. Téa screamed, heard it echoed back from the monster, only stopping when her back slammed against something solid, the breath knocked out of her. Gasping like a fish out of water, she scanned her surroundings, recognized them. How the hell had she gotten here? Still struggling, she turned to look at Leif, leaning against the same wall a few lockers down. Without saying a word, he leapt to his feet and went around the corner. Finally drawing a deep breath, Téa stood, wondering what to do next.

"Check all the doors, there's gotta be a way out," Leif commanded as he came back around the corner and ran off down the hallway. She frowned. What was he talking about? There were exit doors all over the school. They'd be locked of course, but only against people coming in. They should still be able to get out.

Turning the same corner Leif had, she tried each one of the four doors that formed a metal and glass wall. Locked!

"No, that's not right!" She pushed the doors, pulled, shook them, but they didn't budge. They were locked in.

But why? And how? This was all just a vision, wasn't it?

She wandered through labyrinths of corridors, feeling like a rat in a maze, trying to gather her thoughts. There had been the broken glass, then the cut on her finger that had brought the blood. Blood, the vision, and not Gate, but Leif. Why? Despite the lack of a marking, Gate made so much more sense. Didn't he? Téa thought so. On the other hand, Leif did have the mark. What was the reason she and he both had the same symbol on opposite arms?

A pulsing began in the crook of her left arm. She lifted it to look at the mark. It glowed, throbbed with the beat of her heart. For a moment, she just watched it, then lightly swept her right hand over it. Although the symbol felt no different, as her fingers touched on it, she heard voices. Disconcerted, she dropped both arms back to her sides. What was that? She wiggled her fingers, considering whether or not to do it again.

Deciding not to, she set off down the hallway again. Whatever was happening had something to do with those damn tattoos, but would listening to a bunch of what sounded like random voices really help?

Her sneakers made a resounding squeak on the floor as she stopped and sniffed the air. Staleness, yet fresh at the same time, like after a rainstorm but with a muddy scent beneath. Had there been any smells when they first landed? She tried to recall but couldn't remember. Was that simply because it didn't register or because there weren't any smells?

She reached the office. A metal screen was pulled across the counter. Out of curiosity, she tried the pale wooden entrance door that read "OFFICE." Locked of course. But shouldn't that sign read "PRIN-CIPAL'S OFFICE"? She looked closer. There was no indication that anyone had removed or replaced anything. She ran her fingers over the gold and black stick-on sign. Above it. Below it.

Smooth.

Strange.

Eerie silence pressed in, loud in her ears. A chill shivered along her spine.

Backing away from the door, she quickened her pace and headed for the stairs that led up to the cafeteria.

Leif stood at the top putting money in the pop machine, then waited for his prize. Since when did he dress down like that? Baggy blue tee, loose jeans and bare feet. She supposed he hadn't expected to wind up in a vision. But why was his hair still perfectly gelled? Did he sleep with it that way?

A can rumbled into the machine's pocket. He took it, popped the tab and took a long drink. She climbed the stairs. If he heard her, he paid no attention. She cleared her throat.

He turned, a sort of spaced-out look on his face as he stared at her.

She asked him if he was going to share.

He looked at the can as if it held all the answers.

She wished it did. Wanting to rip the can from his fingers and swallow the liquid that was left inside, she instead shook her head and stalked past him, fingers curled into her palms.

Maybe she shouldn't have felt so angry, but it seemed communicating with Leif was going to be a problem, just like it had been at the McDonald's downtown. Only now he was just acting dumb. Whether it was because of her or because he was in some kind of denial, sooner or later they would need to talk to one another.

Chapter Six—The Thing in the Cafeteria

If he lifted his head, Leif could have seen the entire cafeteria. Not that it mattered; there was nothing special there. With arms lying crossed on a table and his forehead propped on them, he stared at the floor. For the first time he realized his feet were bare. How could he have walked across the cold tile floor of the school and the laminated wood floor in the gym and not realized he wasn't wearing any shoes—it made no sense. But then, dreams never did, and wasn't that all visions really were? Just dreams?

But why Téa? He had no personal interest in her. And what was with those tattoos on their arms? Had it been something trendy the years they'd been born, to get your baby tattooed? Had they gone together after Téa's birth? Why not Jeremy then? Birthmark? Not likely, no matter what his parents claimed. He rolled his eyes trying to see the mark, but it wasn't clear from this awkward position.

He finally lifted his head. With only a glance now for the crook of his right arm, he looked around the cafeteria. Téa had been here a few minutes ago, sitting at another table, chin in her hands, eyes closed. Now she was gone again.

Sun shone in through the long windows along one wall. Yet it was snowing. He frowned. Hadn't it been raining? He'd heard it beating on the roof of his house. "I must have fallen back to sleep," he said to himself.

Wait a minute! Could he get out through those windows? He started to get up, but realized they were just large panes of solid glass, no screens or any way to open them. Some of the upper floor windows had sliders, but was the jump worth it?

Jump? It slowly dawned on him that all he really needed to do was wake up. Hadn't he heard once that you couldn't die in your dreams because, if you did, you'd die in real life? Or something like that. He could wiggle out an upstairs window, jump and wake himself up. But what if he *did* die inside this dream?

With a sigh, he sat back down, then poked at the inside of his arm. "Come on, Leif, wake up."

The counsellors' offices! They also had sliders, locked only from the inside by a little plastic locking mechanism. Easy enough to open and slip out to the ground merely feet or inches beneath the sill. He rose, looked around for Téa, shrugged when he didn't see her, then headed for the offices.

In the first of three offices, he walked around a big oak desk to the double-paned glass. Three smaller panes crossed the bottom. Leif flicked open one of the latches and tried to slide the window back. It didn't budge. He tried again. Still nothing.

Turning, he scanned the desk for something to break the latch with. Or maybe even the window. A stone paperweight/pen holder sat on top of a few pieces of looseleaf with writing on them. He grabbed it, dumped the pens and pencils out, then slammed it against plastic and glass. The latch broke off, but the window stayed intact. He tried to slide the window again. Nothing. As he reached to pick up the stone, he noticed something.

Shielding his eyes against the glare of the sun, he watched snowflakes drifting down and disappearing once they hit the ground. He gazed across the parking lot to the track circling the field behind the school. A lone runner, probably trying to run his way to health, jogged around the route as if everything were normal. But somehow, the sunlight was all wrong. Then he knew. There was no warmth on his face.

Moving his arm, he looked up to the sky and saw that it wasn't the sun shining at all, but the moon. How could the moon be shining that bright, lighting everything as if it were day? The jogger didn't seem to notice.

"Hey," he yelled, banging on the window with the hand not holding the paperweight. "Hey, can you hear me?"

Don't be stupid, he told himself, of course he can't. "Why won't anyone wake me up?"

Going back to the desk, he lifted the stone and threw it against the larger main window. It clunked on the glass and dropped uselessly to the floor.

He cursed and slapped his hands on the top of the desk.

"Leif?"

He spun around. Téa stood there, eyes wide, leaning against the doorframe, looking terrified and every bit as confused as he felt.

# # #

Téa looked in the girls' washroom mirror while she washed her hands. She wasn't dressed much better than Leif: Loose-fitting, white lounge pants with "girl power" in black down the left leg, and an over-sized black, long-sleeved tee that said "girl power" in white letters. Her parents had given them to her last year for Christmas.

"I picked them out," Dad had said proudly. Which, of course, set her mother off.

The pajamas were a size too big, which Téa preferred, but had he known that, or was he just unaware of the size she wore. She hadn't bothered listening to the argument to find out, and no one asked her opinion.

Her long hair stuck out like she'd eaten electricity for breakfast, and her eyeliner was smudged. She used a paper towel to wipe most of it off, leaving a thin black line on her lower lid. She shrugged. Whatever. There was no one here to care.

"Same as usual," she said to her image.

Then her stomach growled. When was the last time she'd eaten? Her McDonald's meal with Darla? No, that had been Friday. Today was Saturday. Maybe. For all she knew it was Sunday, Monday, or even an entire week later.

That thought should have terrified her a lot more than it did. But the sweet relief from the chaos at home tempered the panic. She slumped against the wall, then slid down to the floor and closed her eyes, trying to focus on nothing, just clear her mind. But too many thoughts crowded in, questions wanting answers.

What was the connection between her and Leif besides the marks on their arms? Why were they at the school? Most importantly, how were they going to get out of there, wherever "there" was?

She took a long, deep breath. "Come on, Téa," she reprimanded herself. "If you can deal with Mom and Dad, you can deal with this and figure it out."

Although it creeped her out, she placed her fingers on her arm and forced herself to listen carefully, to try to understand what the voices said.

It was impossible to pick just one to concentrate on, but she managed to identify a few familiar voices: her mother, her father, Aunt Darla and . . . Gate? She yanked her fingers away at the shock. Gate? "Dammit!" Still no idea what was being said, just another question raised.

With a sigh, she got to her feet, her sneakers making little squeaking sounds on the tiled floor. Maybe she could find a bag of chips or a chocolate bar in the cafeteria kitchen. Instead, she found something horrifyingly riveting.

Beneath plastic sneeze guards, in the metal warming trays, a feast was displayed. Scents of chicken, vegetables, and gravy wafted through the air. A finger of fear poked Téa in the chest. Roasted chicken was what Gate had thought he smelled! Gate again, a small voice in her head said. So why was Leif here?

A robed figure, face hidden beneath a hood, stood there as though admiring its work. Téa's stomach growled again, and the creature looked up as if it had heard.

It looked like something from a horror movie, not her school or anyone's school. Standing frozen, her heart pounding, blood rushing in her ears, Téa saw that the face beneath the hood wasn't a single face, and yet it was. The faces of her parents and Leif's rippled and blended across features that both were and weren't there. Other faces appeared, blurred, so Téa wasn't sure who they were. Gate? Darla? Atlas? What did it all mean?

Somehow, through her fear, Téa realized that sometimes the features didn't match. Her mother's eyes, Leif's curls. Her father's nose, her chin, and many other combinations, no two the same, some not even familiar to her.

Finally, the thing spoke. "What do you want, child? Choose." The voice didn't belong to anyone she knew. Rasping, cigarette-smoker rough, neither male nor female.

Chills cramped her muscles at the sound, and Téa backed away. Skidding as if on oil-slicked tiles, she scrambled out of the kitchen, ran through the cafeteria, past the pop machine where'd she'd seen Leif earlier, and nearly fell down the stairs. She didn't stop until she reached the hallway where the counsellors' offices were. Hands on knees, heart racing, she gulped air. What the hell was that thing?

"Hey! Hey, can you hear me?"

Leif? Who was he talking to? Her?

She headed down the hall. A thunk, then a dull thud identified which office he was in. Peering in, she saw him slap his hands against the desk, his curse accenting his frustration.

"Leif?"

He turned. His eyes, reflecting her own confusion, locked onto hers.

Chapter Seven—Jeremy's Dream

"What are you doing?" Leif shrieked at her, flapping his arms at his sides.

She gulped, hands curling into fists at her sides, belly muscles trembling. What was he so mad at? She cleared her throat, hoping for a steady voice when she spoke.

"There's something in the cafeteria I think you should see. And why are you yelling at me?"

He looked at her as if trying to comprehend what she was telling him, like he had to decipher some kind of ancient code. Finally, he shook his head and spoke. No apology, but softer this time. "There's something right here *you* need to see." He jabbed a finger at the window.

She slid her eyes in that direction, saw nothing except the glare of the fluorescent lighting in the ceiling. But a glance upward showed her that the lights weren't even on. She wished Darla were here, or even Jeremy. Someone more comforting than Leif was.

"It's dark out there," she mumbled, "but it's daylight in here."

He frowned. "What? No––" He broke off and turned back toward the window. "Don't you see the sun? I mean the moon."

Going back to the window, he looked out and tapped it with his finger. "There's a dude running out there on the track in full daylight! It's daylight because the *moon* is shining, and it's snowing!" His voice rose as he spoke, but after a pause, he'd composed himself again. "Look, I know weird things happen in dreams, but this is just so, so weird."

So weird? It was definitely more than weird. But Téa understood that the situation was so overwhelming he had no words to adequately describe it.

"Tell me about it," she said then went to the glass, cupped her hands on it and peered out. The dusk-to-dawn lights in the parking lot and around the track had come on, but there wasn't any running guy, nor any snow. Then something caught her eye. She dropped her hands and backed away from the window, stumbling into the chair at the desk.

Leif reached out and caught her arm before she could fall. "What's wrong?"

Pulling out the chair to sit, she said, "You said something about the moon."

"Yeah, it's shining like the sun."

"No, Leif." She shook her head. "Look again."

He glanced out the window. "Téa, it's super bright, but it's still just the moon."

Breathing deep, she struggled to stay calm and not freak out. "It has the mark on it," she said touching her arm through her sleeve. "This mark."

He frowned deeply and looked like he might yell again. Téa wrapped her arms over her chest. But he didn't yell.

Instead, he squinted as he looked out the window. "I don't see that, Téa."

He turned back to her and once again looked into her eyes with mounting confusion. "What's happening?" His voice was soft. There was something else in his eyes––what was it?

Eye contact suddenly became uncomfortable, creepy. She tore her gaze away, looked at her shoes. "I don't know."

An uneasy silence lingered for too long. Then he broke it.

"Didn't you want to show me something?" he asked, kinder than she'd expected.

She met his intense gaze. What was it about those eyes? She opened her mouth to speak, but realized there wasn't much point now showing him the thing in the cafeteria, not if they weren't seeing the same things. On the other hand, what he did see might be useful in getting them out. She couldn't fathom how, but at this point, she was willing to try anything.

"Yeah. Come on."

He followed her most of the way in silence, but as they slowed near the cafeteria kitchen, he asked, "Are we both having the same dream at the same time?"

"Something like that," she said, pulling in a deep breath, working up the courage to face that thing again. She didn't want to argue about what exactly was happening until she made him look. It was a long, probably impossible shot, but if what he saw could stop this, they wouldn't need to talk about it. They could just go about their lives the same as before.

Peering in, she saw the figure was still there diligently working. "Look in there."

He did as she asked, then gaped at her as though she'd lost her mind. "It's just the cafeteria lady." His voice was laced with frustration, but no edge now.

Téa's mind whirled as she considered what to say to him. What would make the most sense? Or did it even matter?

"Okay look, who's she cooking all that food for? There's no one here but us."

"She's not cooking. She's cleaning."

Cleaning? That made more sense, but why didn't she see that? Leif was staring at her, as if searching for an answer in her face. Did he even believe her? What if she went in the kitchen and grabbed some food?

That thing though, with its freaky face, was terrifying. She glanced at it again. It seemed to be minding its own business now, but how close could she get before it glowered at her, spoke to her again, or did something worse?

She took a tentative step. Then another.

"What are you doing?" Leif asked.

Hand up, palm facing him, she signaled for silence. If she was going to do this, she didn't want the thing to have any warning. It didn't look up, didn't stop its actions.

A few more steps. Still, it didn't seem to notice.

Finally, she reached the display of food and grabbed a plate from the stack. Pause. No reaction. She piled on potatoes, carrots and chicken. Added a roll. Smothered the whole thing with gravy. Grabbed a fork. Ran on tiptoes back to Leif.

She held it out to him, like an offering to a god. His jaw dropped as he stared at the plate resting on her palms. "Where did that come from?"

"I told you, she's cooking. A lot of food. A whole feast."

He sniffed.

"What? Do you think I'm trying to poison you or something?"

"It smells weird."

She held the plate toward him. "Taste it."

Again, he did as she asked. Scooping potato and gravy with the fork, he sniffed again, then popped it into his mouth. Grimaced. "Tastes disgusting." He spat, handed the plate back to her, then glanced in the creature's direction.

"It's right there," said Téa. "Right in front of you. Do you see it now?"

"There's nothing in there except an old woman with rags and cleaner," he insisted.

Frustrated, she flung plate, food and fork to the ground, then immediately regretted it. She hadn't even tasted it to see if he was right. Just because it smelled good didn't mean it tasted good. And just because he said it tasted weird didn't mean it did. Would they taste things differently too?

Food splattered and the plate broke in two. The fork clattered across the floor. Téa glanced at whoever it was in the cafeteria. It glanced up, as if it had heard. She took a step back, but it went right back to work.

"Why don't you ask her to help us get out of here?" she blurted.

He glared at her and, for a moment, everything seemed to spin around them. A lock of hair fell over Leif's forehead in slow motion, and for a moment he looked bizarrely like her father. His lips were moving, but she couldn't hear what he was saying. She closed her eyes.

Why couldn't it have been Gate she was connected to? Even Jeremy. Either one of them would have been a better companion right now.

The spinning sensation became worse, unsettling. Some-one--Leif?--touched her arm. The world slowed to a crawl. Her eyes opened in the same sluggish manner Leif's hair had fallen. Leif was no longer in front of her.

The delicious aroma of warm food tickled her nose and made her stomach growl again. When she looked in that direction, Leif was standing in the middle of the kitchen. Just standing there. Doing nothing except muttering. "It doesn't make any sense at all. Nothing makes any sense." He scrubbed at his face with his hands.

Ignoring his protests, she went in and grabbed another plate. She was starving! But as she served herself more food, she wondered if this food actually had substance. Could she eat it and feel full, or could she just keep eating, never filling up? And which one would make this all make more sense?

The smell of food was faint, but it was there. Watching Téa stuff food into her mouth, Leif tried to comprehend what was happening. At first, he smelled nothing but pine cleaner, even when Téa brought the plate to him. The potatoes tasted like blood and mildew to him--obviously not to her.

After Téa suggested asking the cleaning lady (wasn't her name Kathy?) to help them, he went to do just that. Although it came out of nowhere, it seemed like a good idea. Before he entered the cafeteria, though, Téa paled as though she were sick. When she closed her eyes, her body sagged, and he thought she *was* going to be sick. He asked her but got no response. Not even when he touched her.

So, he went into the kitchen only to find Kathy gone. The entire room was dark and empty. He figured she must have slipped out when he wasn't looking and was now on her way home. Which was exactly where he should have been. Home. In bed. But that's where he was already, wasn't it? He pressed his fingers against his aching forehead. Was he going crazy, or was this just one of the wildest dreams he'd ever had? "This has got to be a dream, *our* dream, doesn't it?"

Pausing with fork halfway between the plate and her mouth, Téa looked at him, blinked. Popped the food in her mouth, then scraped the last of the potatoes and gravy off the plate and swallowed. "Right before this happened, I was cleaning up broken glass. I cut my finger. Then I was in the vision, but it was different. Then I was here. You?"

He thought a moment, his memory fuzzy. There had been rain when he awoke and. And what? His knife. Something about his knife. Then he remembered. Laying his arm on the table, he looked at the mark. No cuts, no nicks, nothing.

"Dammit, Téa! I cut my arm this morning and now look!"

"How?" she asked, as if it mattered. "And why?" She raised her finger to inspect, then showed it to him. "Look, same here. No cut."

He looked at her finger for longer than necessary, his mind whirling. "I, well, I don't know why. I just used a knife." More memories filled in as he spoke. "Yeah, my vision was different too. I think. I don't know. I was there, then I was here."

"We're inside our visions," she said flatly, but with a little grin as if she'd figured out an important secret. Maybe she had. But could it really be?

"Inside? Are you serious?" It made no sense, yet it made perfect sense.

She nodded.

"So, are we missing from our houses? I mean are our bodies gone?"

"I have no idea."

"So how do we get out?"

"If I knew that, do you think I'd stay here? I was hoping Kathy could have helped with that."

"She's gone now."

Grabbing her plate and fork, she headed toward the table where students left their plates for Kathy and the other kitchen staff to gather and wash. He shook his head.

"We can't be 'inside' our visions. That's ridiculous!"

"Any more ridiculous than having the damn things at all? Do you have a better theory?"

He didn't respond. There had to be a better answer, he just had to find it. He pushed away from the table.

"Where are you going?" She deposited the plate, then leaned against the table, watching him.

"I don't know yet."

He went into the hall, looking for something, anything that might give him a clue. The pop machine. He'd put money into it earlier. Realization shot through him like adrenaline. He tingled all over. If it was a dream, he wouldn't have needed money. Maybe the money was just some symbolic dream thing.

He stalked up to the machine and jabbed one of the big rectangular buttons, hoping a can would rattle into the pocket below. That would prove this was nothing more than a dream. Pop wasn't free.

Nothing happened.

"Dammit!" He punched the machine, then leaned his head against it in defeat.

Money clattered into the return slot. Sticking his finger in, Leif pulled out his loonie, or *a* loonie anyway. The same amount of money he'd put in earlier. He stared at the golden coin. It looked real, felt real. He slid it into the slot. This time something happened. He looked at the Coke can, sitting in the machine's pocket. The coin rattled into the return slot. For the third time he deposited his money. Another can appeared beside the first. He sighed deeply. Things like that happened in dreams, didn't they? This couldn't be the vision. Téa couldn't be right. So much confusion.

"Hey! Look at this."

He spun to scan the cafeteria. Long orange tables, yellow plastic chairs, but no Téa.

"Where are you now?"

"In here. The Games Room."

The Games Room! A little room off the cafeteria where all the geeks hung out to play Minecraft, or whatever it was they did in there.

Going to the door, he looked inside. CDs stood in stacks on a table, along with a CD player. A couple of small boxes holding old vinyl had been slid underneath, awaiting the day that format's popularity would be resurrected. Leif knew some people who were into those old, scratchy records. They even had players for them. He was certain they'd have loved to search those boxes.

A small, flat-screen TV sat on another table. Beside it was a small pile of DVDs. A bunch of strange looking equipment was piled, forgotten, in a corner. Several computers, both desktops and laptops, lined another table. None of them were running. Apparently, this was really The Junk Room, hoarding stuff from all the way back when the school had been new. "What's going on?"

Téa stood in a corner, fixated on something, but stepped back to show him a large, old-fashioned floor model television. Was the room like this in real life? He'd never taken an interest in checking, so he had no idea.

A fuzzy black and white image on its glass screen appeared to be a person in a bed, a round white moon shining down, giving the scene an ethereal appearance.

"These old black and white movies are hilarious. Why do they even have this old mammoth in here? Is this really what the room is like?"

"No idea. But, um, Leif?"

He turned to her, then gave a start. She was holding the cord in her hand. The set wasn't even plugged in.

"Talk to me," shouted a voice from the TV at the same time. A chill shivered down Leif's spine as he whipped his head back to the screen. That was Jeremy's voice.

Leif backed away, then plonked into a plastic chair he hadn't even known was there. Suddenly the faint smell of a chicken dinner wafted in and set his stomach to rumbling. He ignored it as his heart began to pound harder, faster. "What the hell?"

"Leif, what's going on?" called Jeremy, sounding confused, concerned.

"You can see me?"

"Yeah, I can see you," said Jeremy as if Leif were an idiot.

"Where are you?"

"I'm still in bed, sleeping."

"Then this *is* a dream?" Leif glanced at Téa, who stood by the door, arms wrapped across her chest.

"Yeah, *my* dream," Jeremy answered.

"*Your* dream? Well, what are you dreaming about?"

"Watching you be stupid on TV," scoffed Jeremy. It seemed there was nothing unreal about him.

Leif frowned. If they were in Jeremy's dream, why were they so aware of it? Why did some things seem real, others bizarre?

"Hey, I gotta go. Mom's yellin', wakin' me up."

"Yes, wake up, please do!"

Then Jeremy was gone and there was only the black screen. Leif waited. Nothing happened. He slapped the top of the television set.

"What's going on?" he demanded, without turning around, hand still on the set.

Chapter Eight—Back to the Basement

Téa took a breath to calm her jitters, and wondered what Jeremy had to do with anything? He didn't have a mark and yet *he* was dreaming about *them*. "We can't be in his dream," she said. "If we were, we'd both see the same things, the things his mind is creating. We wouldn't be so aware either."

Leif swiped at the loose curl dangling in his face. "But he said ––"

"Yeah, he said your mom was waking him up. Don't you think Jeremy's awake by now?" she argued. "And we're still here." She showed him the TV cord again. "How were we even seeing anything on the screen? It's not his dream, it's our vision."

Leif's eyes flashed. Anger, fear, confusion. He remained silent as he stared at the cable in her hand.

"Don't you think I wanted it to be his dream too?" she asked. "But it's not, and we have to figure out what it means."

"How?" he asked, propping his elbows on his knees, his chin in his hands.

"I don't know. But I'll bet it's going to take more than waking up to get us out of here. I'm going to the library. Maybe I can find some books on dreams and visions that will help." She headed for the door.

"Wait," said Leif suddenly, grabbing her arm and standing.

"What?" She tugged her arm loose.

He scratched the blond scruff on his chin. Téa held his gaze. What did he want? He shook his head. "I remember something."

"What?"

"I could never see your face before. This time I did. And the colours covered *us* this time. Both of us."

"The colours connected us. But why?"

The silence that ensued was less awkward than before. Then Téa had an idea. She pulled up her sleeve. "Touch it."

"No!" He brushed at the lock of hair again, but it refused to stay out of his face.

"I'm serious. Go ahead," she encouraged him.

Wincing, he slid his finger onto the red mark on her arm. Almost immediately he yanked it away as though it burned. "What *was* that?"

"You heard the voices, didn't you?"

"Yes."

"Let me touch yours. Have you tried?"

A shake of his head, then he lifted his right arm to her. Placing her finger on his mark, she heard the same garbled voices. "You try." Her voice was almost a whisper as she removed her finger.

"The same." She almost didn't hear him.

"So, there are voices now," she muttered to herself. Then to Leif she said, "Let's try something."

She extended her arm, mark exposed. "I know this sounds weird but put your arm next to mine."

The air around them seemed to chill. Téa looked at him and saw no reaction. He only gazed back expectantly at her. But it was like they were the only two left on earth. Nothing else seemed to exist. Nothing else seemed to matter.

"Touch my arm and I'll touch yours," she said, aware of how sensual it sounded, surprised at the tone of her voice.

Leif shook his head.

"I'm not asking you for sex." Despite her desire to scoff at him or yell, her voice remained that same low, easy tone.

He still didn't move, so she took his other hand to place it on her arm. He shook her off, then curled all the fingers of his left hand back so only his pointer remained on her red spot.

She touched his. How silly they must have looked. Or did it look more exotic, like some kind of Kama Sutra pose? The thought sickened her; she pushed it away.

Voices, muffled and distant, rang in her ears. She looked to Leif. He caught her gaze and nodded. Their fingers and the skin inside their elbows turned icy. Téa shivered, tried to focus on the words. This time she couldn't make out a single word or identify a single voice.

Then the lights dimmed. The cafeteria and the Games Room turned dark with a scarlet glow. Although she still couldn't understand a word being spoken, she knew someone was arguing, recognized the angered tones. Somewhere someone cried.

She had to fight the impulse to curl her right hand into a fist. Leif's finger cold-burned into her skin. Her heart hammered in her chest.

The aroma of food from the kitchen flared strong for a moment, then became an acrid burnt scent.

"Take her," shouted a clear, loud voice through the muffled others. Téa jumped at the sound. She had no idea who had spoken. She looked at Leif, his face bloody and evil in the crimson glow. His eyes shone like two red moons.

Téa gasped and pulled herself away from him, breaking all contact. The light and Leif's face became normal again.

"What happened?" he cried.

Insides quivering, Téa hugged her arms around herself, fingers curled tightly into self-soothing fists. "They were arguing," she said, her voice quivery like she might cry, though she didn't feel it. "Some-one yelled 'Take her.' Didn't you hear it?"

"I heard, but they said, 'Take him.'" His voice sounded panicky. "Who are *they,* and what do they want from us?"

She shrugged, not trusting herself to speak.

He reached out to her, laid his hand on her arm, her sleeve now covering it again. "I think I understand now," he said. "I mean, I don't understand any of this, but if we work together, they can't hurt us."

She snapped her head up to look at him. Was he serious? "How? What did you see?"

He scrunched up his nose. "How what?"

"How did you figure it out?"

"I'm not sure. When the lights went down, you had this, this face like a bloated white moon. An evil white moon."

She nodded. "You were red and scary looking."

"There have to be answers here somewhere," said Leif. "Whatever is going on must have something to do with the school. Why else would we be locked in here?"

"I think that's the most sensible thing you've said so far." She put up her hand to stay his reply. It wasn't a dig; he actually made sense for once. "Well, there are no answers here in the cafeteria," she said. "What about the gym?"

Leif shivered. "Don't go there," he said, then shook his head when she gave him a quizzical look. "Don't even ask. Weren't you going to go to the library before?"

"Yeah, but now I don't think there's anything in there that will help us."

"Why not? Don't libraries have tons of information? You seemed pretty interested in ours."

"That was when I knew what I was looking for. I have no idea now. I need more clues."

Once, she would have gone to the library and happily read every single book she could get her hands on. Even now the peace and quiet it offered was a desirable option, just not a logical one. What was logical though?

"Okay, so what about the basement?" Leif suggested.

"Yes! That's it!" She snapped her fingers. Why hadn't she thought of that? "You may just be a genius after all." She raced from the room and headed toward the kitchen again, skidding to a stop as she neared the door, remembering that even if this door wasn't locked, the stairs were broken.

"What are you waiting for? Let's go."

"We can't use the stairs. They're broken."

"What? How do you know that?" He reached for the knob, twisted and pulled. It came open easily in his hand. He leaned in and she heard a snap as he flipped a light switch. "They look fine to me."

Apparently, anything was possible right now.

"What made you think the stairs were broken?"

She wasn't ready yet to tell him about her little impromptu, breaking-school-rules jaunt with Gate. "This isn't right, Leif."

He'd gone down a few steps and turned to look at her. "Of course it's not right. I know it and you know it."

His voice held a hint of annoyance, but he didn't press her for a real answer about the stairs.

"Come on!" he said.

Having no idea what to expect this time, she slowly followed his lead.

# # #

Doorways dotted a long hallway in the cool, semi-lighted basement. They looked like doors to classrooms, but Leif knew there were no classes down here. Not in his real-life school anyway.

Fluorescent light spilled out from each of the open doors, bright stripes in an otherwise dark, shadowy hallway, looking like Jack-o'-lantern teeth slashed across the floor. A musty odour hung heavy in the air, but Leif swore there was an underlying scent. Chicken?

Eerie footfalls echoed on the wooden stairs. If he didn't know it was Téa, he might have fled. To where, he didn't know, but he wouldn't have stuck around. What made her think the stairs were broken? He started to repeat his question when she sidled up next to him, asking her own question in a whisper. "What now?"

He jumped.

"Did I scare you?"

"No, this place is just kind of eerie." It was the truth. He knew she was coming but hadn't expected her to get so close to him and speak. Her hand brushed against his, slid into it. Startled again, he started to speak but stopped. Somehow the gesture felt right.

They headed down the hall. He stopped as he spied what looked to be an elevator shaft. A long, wide sheet of plastic hung at the other end of the hall, decorated with spatters of red paint. He wasn't even aware the school had an elevator. Hope renewed, he said "Hey, maybe we can get out that way."

"Are you crazy? How is an elevator going to get us out of our visions? Besides, elevators don't lead outside, only to other floors."

Dejected, he still had to admit she had a point. But where did it go, and why wasn't there access to it in reality? Letting go of her hand, he approached it anyway. He wanted to make absolutely sure there was nothing useful this elevator could do for them.

"Forget about it, Leif. It's no use to us. Come on, let's just see what else we can find."

The plastic curtain fluttered as he drew near, snapping lightly. Leif paused then reached out and yanked it aside. A black, empty abyss stared back at him.

"See anything?" Téa asked.

He jumped yet again and leapt backwards. This place really had him on edge. Spinning around to face her at the same time, he stumbled over his own feet and landed on his ass. Téa snorted and let out a chuckle, but she did offer him a hand.

"There's not even an elevator there," he said as he stood. "Just an empty shaft."

"Let's just see what else we can find."

Téa didn't object when he took the lead and walked to the first door. Inside, students sat at wooden desks. A teacher at the front of the class, with her hair pulled into a tight bun and wearing a close-fitting grey skirt and matching jacket, had her back to them as she wrote on a blackboard, SHEARWOOD: A HISTORY.

"Leif," Téa hissed, moving in beside him. "Look!" She nodded toward the words on the board.

"Yeah, what about it?" he murmured.

"That's the name of the book I borrowed from your library."

Shock pulsed through him, body tingling again. He wondered how Téa was feeling right now.

She poked his ribs. "Look at them, at the students. They look old."

"Old? Téa, they're teenagers."

"No, I mean like old-fashioned. Look at their clothes."

He peered closer. The girls wore long, pastel-coloured skirts, cashmere V-neck sweaters, and upswept hair. Guys wore leather jackets and white T-shirts with cigarette packages rolled up in the sleeves. Most with hair slicked back on the sides and curled into a swirl in the middle of their foreheads. Some of them wore glasses, black square ones for the guys and round with a point at each temple for the girls. His grandmother used to have a pair like that when he was little. What were they called? Cat's ears or something strange like that.

"Now, class," the teacher began and turned to the students.

Téa uttered a little cry. Leif gasped. Instead of a face, the teacher had what looked like swirls of moon-lit mist.

"Oh, come in, children," she said in a pleasant voice emitting from the moon mist. It was impossible to tell whether she was talking to Leif and Téa. Her non-face seemed to take in the whole room at once. "Don't be afraid."

Leif glanced at Téa. Her eyes were wide, but it wasn't quite fear shining in them. It was there, but something else as well. Was this exciting for her?

"Yes, you two. Leif and Téa Smith. Class, please be kind and welcome our new students."

Leif and Téa Smith? Leif almost corrected her, telling her he wasn't a Smith, he was a Noble. But how did she even know their names?

Téa grabbed his hand and pulled him into the room. The students had all turned to stare at them. At least they had normal-looking faces.

"Do you really think we should?" he asked, plodding along behind Téa, resisting slightly.

"What else are we going to do? Run away?"

"It might have been a better choice," he hissed.

Téa chose one of two empty seats near the front on the far side of the room, and sat, pointing at the one beside it. "We might learn something in here."

So, that was why she seemed so eager. She even appeared to be interested in what the teacher was droning on about. Leif couldn't even look at the woman. He observed the students instead. They returned their gazes to the faceless one and never moved or made a sound.

"Téa, did you finish reading this last night?" The teacher pointed to the title on the blackboard.

"Uh, um, yeah. Yeah, I did."

Leif held his breath, waiting to see what would happen next. She said she'd borrowed it, but it wasn't last night, was it? And did she finish it?

"What did you learn?" asked the teacher.

"Shearwood has a history of cults and––"

The teacher frowned. "No, that's not right. Téa Smith, go to the office at once," she commanded.

Téa obviously didn't need to be told twice. Her face fell as she jumped up and scrambled out of the class. Well, that didn't last very long, Leif thought as he grabbed his chance and bounded along behind her, wondering if she'd learned anything at all. It didn't seem so to him.

In the hall, Leif glanced back into the room. He saw nothing except thin moon-lit fog rising from the floor.

Chapter Nine—Wet Paint

Téa had never been more thankful to be sent to the office than this time; she'd almost expected the horrifying faceless thing to chase them. When nothing happened, it occurred to her that maybe they couldn't get hurt inside the vision.

Though this version of the basement was still creepy, it wasn't as bad as it was when she'd been here in reality. Where did this elevator go, and why were the stairs intact? And, she wondered for the first time, who went to the basement in reality? Who besides Atlas knew about that elevator?

She peered into a classroom and, finding it empty, wondered what it had been before. Would the ones she and Gate entered be identifiable here?

In the next room, desks were piled with books. Dust coated everything. Boxes, wardrobes, and broken gym equipment filled another room. One of the wardrobe doors hung open revealing fancy Victorian clothing inside. Probably costumes for school plays. Puzzling.

Had these been classrooms prior to moving the Meeting Hall down here? Why bother moving it then? Of course, this place wasn't necessarily reflecting the real school. Some parts of it were, but others were off, a twisted version. With that in mind, she wondered where they might have ended up if they'd been able to leave the school. Would they step back into reality or just more of the warped variety?

What *was* Shearwood like outside these particular walls? Would there be more people without faces? Would they experience events that never happened? She almost wished they could get out just so she could see, so she could test her theory about not getting hurt.

"I don't think we should go into any more rooms," said Leif.

Aware that he'd been following her, she turned to face him, eyebrows raised, arms crossed over her chest. "Why not? Just because we didn't learn anything in there doesn't mean we won't in another room." She resisted asking him if he was scared. Of course he was. Who wouldn't be? They still had to check things out though, see what they could learn. They couldn't just sit and do nothing.

He flapped his hand in the general direction of the class they'd come from while scoffing and reminding her how creepy it had been. She reminded him that they weren't hurt, then told him what she thought. He seemed to accept her theory then got all wound up about something in the room. "What about that?" he asked.

She watched his fingers slide through his sticky, dirty hair as he blew out a breath. Did he really care about his perfect curls right now? No, she decided, he probably just wanted a shower, and she understood that. How strange was this? She actually "got" Leif Noble.

She shook her head. "What about what? We already established––"

"I meant, there was mist in there, Téa. Don't bother coming to look, it's gone now."

"I probably wouldn't have seen it anyway." She whirled around and started down the hall again through the bars of light.

"Wait a second! Maybe you would have. We both saw Jeremy and we both saw the same thing in that class. What does it mean?"

She grinned without turning around. "So, blond playas do have a few brain cells, eh?" A laugh-snort escaped her. She couldn't help that one. It was something she would have even said to Jeremy, if he were blond.

"What's *that* supposed to mean?" he asked, taking it a lot more personal than she thought he would. It wasn't worth commenting on. They both knew what she was suggesting. What she didn't know was why they were suddenly seeing the same things. Could it be significant?

"Téa!" a voice boomed out of nowhere.

She whirled, her own limp, unwashed hair swinging into her face. She scraped it away wishing for a scrunchie.

"Who said that? Leif, was that Jeremy again?" She scanned the hall, searching fervently for his face somewhere, yet terrified she might see something chilling.

Leif said he didn't know. The voice rang out again.

"Téa, come to me. I'm over here."

Leif pulled her close. What the hell was he doing? The warmth of his body against hers was both comforting and revolting. She twisted in his arms, looked up at him. *Does he want to protect me, or me to protect him?*

"Téa, I--" Confusion contorted his face and, for one horrible moment, she thought he might kiss her. The idea nauseated her. She broke away from his grasp.

"What are you doing?" she shrieked, her voice shriller than she'd intended. Her hands clenched into fists almost of their own accord.

His mouth opened, but no sound came out. His cheeks were flushed.

"Téa, please come here." The voice was softer now, and this time she recognized it as Jeremy's. But where was he? She turned away from Leif, and a shimmer in a nearby room caught her eye.

Taking a hesitant step toward it, she looked closer and noticed two things. The first was Jeremy, standing in the corner. The second was that this was the room where Gate had found the paint on the floor. It looked a bit different, but she recognized the pedestal sink and the wooden cupboard with the moons carved into it.

"Jeremy?" she cried. "Jeremy, get us out of here. Wake us up! Do something!"

"Jeremy, what are you doing here?" Leif asked from behind her.

"I'm not really here, you dolt," his brother responded. "Téa, you need to look at me."

"I am."

"More closely."

A shock jolted through her when she did as he asked.

She could see through him! Through his jeans and T-shirt, through his body, she could see the wall behind him. Something that looked like a newspaper clipping was taped to it beside the white sink.

"Yes, you see it, don't you? Look closer still."

She took a deep breath to calm her nerves, her racing heart. She trusted Jeremy. Whatever he wanted her to see had to be important.

She first noticed remains of candles in the sink, and something that looked like a chunk of moldy cake. She snatched the clipping from the wall, quickly scanning the floor. No red paint.

Before looking at the square of paper, she turned her gaze to the shelf. All the bottles were upright, each one filled with a different substance. Some were coloured liquids and others, herbs. Full bottles!

"Téa, you should look at that clipping."

"I will." She looked at the floor again. There had to be paint there.

"What are you looking for?" asked Leif.

"Paint. Red paint."

"Paint?" asked the brothers at the same time.

She moved in small steps. Then she saw it---the faded remains of red paint. Following the outline with her eyes, it looked like it might have been a symbol at one time, but she couldn't tell for sure. Had there been a symbol on the floor in the room she and Gate had entered? Neither of them had thought to check.

"What is she doing?" Jeremy asked.

"I don't know," came his brother's response.

She knelt next to a spot that was less faded and touched her finger to it. Wet paint clung to her skin.

Chapter
Ten—Jeremy's Reality

Warmth from a late fall sun, intensified by the glass in the hospital window, spread over Jeremy as he waited for his parents. Visitors scurried by, and patients in johnny gowns scuffed down the hall, some dragging IV poles. Beeps, blips and announcements over the PA system kept Jeremy from falling into a comfortable sleep. That and the worry he harboured for his brother. Leif was a pain in the ass sometimes, but that didn't mean Jeremy never wanted to see him again. What happened to him this morning anyway?

Although it seemed like forever ago, it had only been this morning he dreamed about Leif and Téa on a TV set in something like a void. The TV screen and the set itself had been clear. But the picture was dark and somewhat foggy, impossible to identify where they were. He knew it had air, though, because he'd been able to breathe. Except it was only a dream, he reminded himself. Part of him understood, though, it was something more. Had to be.

His mother's voice had woken him, but when he opened his eyes, his mother wasn't in his room. He could hear her and his father running through the house, shouting at each other, yelling into a phone. Something about Leif. The chaos eventually led him to his brother's room. Standing in his boxers, he watched, confused, as his mother cried. Both parents leaned over Leif, the phone in Dad's hand slipped to the floor, the 911 operator repeating her question.

Grief rose into Jeremy's throat and his gut clenched. Was Leif dead? He lay so still on his bed. Jeremy scooped up the phone and jabbed his father in the arm with it.

"Dad. Hey, Dad." His voice broke then, so he shoved the phone in front of his father's face. Charles took it, straightened up, and resumed his conversation in a very tight, controlled voice with the operator.

But Leif wasn't dead, only unconscious. Once Elaine realized Jeremy was in the room, she stood and dried her tears. While Dad remained on the phone, Mom drew Jeremy out in the hall and demanded to know if Leif had been a drug user.

"I don't know," Jeremy said with a sniff, trying to hold back his own tears.

"Think, Jeremy," Mom pressed.

Then the memory had broken through the fog in his brain, became as clear as if it had happened just yesterday. But it had been a few months earlier, his last year, last month, of middle school when Leif had come to pick him up.

#

A hard rain poured down, soaking Jeremy as he jumped into the front seat of Leif's car and shook water from his hair.

"Hey, watch where you're spraying that," Leif had reprimanded.

Jeremy grinned and shook his head once more just to annoy his older brother. Then he reached into his jacket pocket and removed what a fellow student had placed there while Jeremy waited for his drive.

All hell broke loose.

"Where'd you get that?" Leif demanded. "Who gave you that joint?"

"Just some guy," Jeremy told him. "Chill, it's only marijuana. I'm gonna flush it anyway."

"You're damn right you are." Leif opened his door, undid his seatbelt and started to get out into the deluge.

"When we get home," Jeremy yelled. "Not now, you dolt!"

With one leg outside the car, Leif glared at him. Then he stuck his finger in Jeremy's face. "First thing when we get there. I want to see you do it."

"Okay, okay." It was only a single joint, and Jeremy didn't understand what the big deal was. He'd never planned on smoking it.

At home, Big Brother grabbed him by the neck and dragged him into the downstairs bathroom.

"Flush it now." Leif pushed him toward the toilet.

"All right. Just chill!"

When the deed was done, Leif shoved him against the wall.

"Don't let me ever catch you with that shit again! If you ever eat, drink, smoke, inject or snort anything, I'll . . . do you remember Mandy?" His reddened face contorted, and Jeremy swore his eyes glowed electric blue.

Mandy! She'd died of an overdose. Now Jeremy understood Leif's anger.

\# \# \#

"No," he said with confidence. "He doesn't do drugs."

"Are you sure?" his mother asked.

He didn't get to answer her question. The wail of sirens pierced the air and sent them running, Charles demanding that Jeremy get dressed. Before he returned to his own room, Jeremy turned back to his unconscious brother. Leif's left arm was exposed, and Jeremy inspected the birthmark, puzzled by the tiny cut slashed across it. What did that even mean?

# # #

Eyes heavy now, he shifted in his seat in the hospital waiting room to find a more comfortable position. He rested his arm on the windowsill, staring outside. There wasn't much to see; the waiting room only looked out on other wings of the hospital. Jeremy laid his head on his arm, trying to ignore the memories, plus the sounds and smells of the hospital. Focussed on the warmth wrapped around him like a hug from the sun, his eyes closed.

With sleep came darkness, like a black hole with air. Jeremy saw Leif and Téa starring in their own movie on a TV screen, black and white like on a surveillance camera. They walked along a hallway that looked vaguely familiar, but Jeremy couldn't place it.

"Téa," he whispered.

The two of them jumped, then Téa whirled around, her hair dull and hanging limp. She pulled it back as if she were going to put it into a ponytail, then let it go again.

"Who said that? Leif, was that Jeremy again?"

"I don't know."

Jeremy watched them, ideas bubbling around his brain like a fragmented dream. Somehow, he knew this was real and yet not real. He could never have explained what this was, or how he felt at that moment, any more than he could explain how big the universe was. He reached out to a large, numbered knob on the TV, knowing it would change the channel even though he'd never even seen a set like this before. The screen flickered as he twisted. When he finally stopped, an empty classroom showed on the screen. *Where is this place? Can I go there?*

He lifted his leg and pushed it toward the screen. The TV offered no resistance. His foot disappeared. And it tingled. Like bugs and adrenaline racing along flesh that was waking up after a long nap.

He stood like that for a moment, wondering if the same thing would happen to him as happened to Leif. Had his brother dreamed of a TV that he climbed into? Had he felt that odd sensation on his body?

Maybe, just maybe, dream-Jeremy reasoned, he'd be able to travel between here and there (wherever there was) because he had no marks. No cuts. Deciding to take a chance, he finished climbing into the television.

Suddenly he blinked, unsure that he was seeing what he thought he was seeing. He was on TV, but he was also watching himself on TV. A sensation stranger than anything he'd ever experienced filled him as he looked around a classroom and watched himself do it at the same time. The surprise at finding himself in some kind of school only added to the feeling. His head whirled, his heart thumped, and he was afraid he might explode. Then there was the smell––a strange blend of blood and cold air.

Get a grip, Jeremy. Focus.

He noticed a newspaper clipping glowing through his chest. Part of him leaned closer to read it, part of him watched. It made him dizzy, so he closed his eyes for a moment. Breathing deep, he talked himself through it. Eyes opened slowly, focussed on a spot in front of him, saw the clipping. Read it. Now that was interesting. Téa was going to love this!

"Téa, come to me. I'm over here."

He waited, brimming with electric excitement. He called out once more, asking her to join him.

A few seconds later, with Leif close behind her, Téa stepped into the room.

"Jeremy?" she cried. "Jeremy, get us out of here. Wake us up! Do something!"

"Jeremy, what are you doing here?" Leif asked from behind her.

"I'm not really here, you dolt." He understood that Leif probably knew that, but he needed Téa to look at him. Somehow, he knew he didn't have long here. Anytime now he could be woken up.

"Téa, you need to look at me. Look at the clipping."

She took a deep breath then passed her hand through him to grab the clipping. He knew he should have been creeped out, but despite everything, he wasn't.

Distracted by something on the floor, Téa apparently didn't feel the electricity or the excitement. Holding the clipping, she walked in tight little circles, as though searching for something.

"Téa, you need to look at that clipping." He'd been certain she would dig right into it. Sure, it wasn't much, but he thought she'd find it interesting, nonetheless.

She looked up at an enclosed shelf, one with moons carved into its sides. All kinds of bottles filled with a variety of things sat on it. "I will." She looked at the floor again. What on earth was she looking for? "Paint," she said when Leif asked that very question.

"Paint?" he and Leif asked at the same time. She didn't answer, just knelt on the floor.

Neither of them had any idea what she was doing. Leif turned to him instead. "Where are you? In reality, I mean?"

"At the hospital. I fell asleep."

"A hospital? Why are you in the hospital?" Panic entered Leif's voice.

"I'm just waiting for Mom and Dad," said Jeremy. "You're in a . . ." He looked at Leif, wondering how much to divulge. Could the situation get worse if the patients knew certain things about themselves?

"I'm in a what?" pressed Leif.

"I don't know if I should tell you."

"Jeremy! Am I still home in bed?" Pleading filled his eyes. Normally Jeremy could ignore Leif's demands. This was different.

"No. You're in a coma," Jeremy finally blurted.

Leif stared at him, frowning. "Oh my god! Is Téa in one too?"

"I don't know."

Fingers scraped through the worst mess of hair Jeremy had ever seen on his brother. He held his breath. *What now?*

"So, this is a dream! Like, a coma dream."

Jeremy shrugged. "I don't know. I don't think so." Would this be possible if Leif were only coma dreaming? How could any of it happen anyway? "All I know is, that in my dream I climbed into a TV set to get here."

"What? How is that possible?"

"Jeremy!" A female voice sounded, somewhere far away. His mother?

He tried to ignore the voice and concentrate on Leif, and whatever Téa was doing, but then the shaking started.

The voice again. More insistent.

He felt himself falling out of the old TV screen.

###

Waking up in a sitting position on the floor, his mother watching over him, her hands on his shoulders, face creased with worry.

"Mom, why am I on the floor?" He looked up into her eyes and couldn't stop the gasp that left his mouth. He faked a yawn to cover it up. Her eyes, honey brown. They looked like, like what? Whatever he'd seen there was gone as quick as it had come. They were his mom's eyes, nothing else.

"You fell off the chair, Jeremy. You frightened me half to death." The look on her face, and the breathiness of her voice told him what she left unsaid. She thought he'd gone into a coma just like Leif.

"Sorry, Mom." Good going, Jer, he thought. What if he'd stayed inside the TV? Didn't his mother have enough to worry about? Yes, he argued with himself, but *I didn't stay in the TV.* And if he could get some answers, maybe he could give his parents some relief until Leif woke up.

Elaine took his hands and helped him to his feet. As his father came around the corner and into the waiting area, Jeremy had a terrible thought. What if Leif and Téa *couldn't* wake up?

"Come, let's go. It's time to go home now," his father said.

"Yes," agreed Elaine, dropping her son's hands. "There's nothing more we can do, and I have my own patients to see in the morning. They'll notify us of any changes."

Every bit of the worry and all the lines had gone from her face. She was the woman of steel once more, caring but cold and stiff with her emotions.

That's your son you're talking about, Jeremy wanted to scream as they chatted about Leif like they were conducting business. His father opened and closed his hands, fiddled with clothing, fingered strands of hair. At least he was showing, however ambiguously, that he felt something. But his mother, Doctor Noble, was always (almost) in tight control.

"They have no idea what's wrong," his father said. Although fear laced his voice, he spoke as though he knew exactly what was wrong and had every right to be scared. Jeremy bit his tongue, not asking what he most wanted to: Why?

Elaine nodded. "Yes, I've had them run all the tests. Nothing's showing up." Her voice broke slightly, she cleared her throat, held her head a little higher.

His parents were firm believers in science and medicine, but they also seemed convinced that most sicknesses and diseases were some sort of punishment. Jeremy hoped they didn't say that to their patients. They'd never said it directly to either him or Leif, but Jeremy had been able to pick up on the idea. Mostly from things they said to one another. Mostly when he heard stuff he didn't think he was supposed to hear.

"There has to be something someone can do to fix it." Jeremy looked at his father waiting for his reply. Not for the first time, he noted how neither he nor Leif had any of his father's looks. Jeremy could see how he looked like his mother, and Leif had her mouth and nose, but that was all. It had never meant anything before. So why now, when his world had been tipped sideways, did it seem so important? He glanced at his mother again. Her eyes. What was it about her eyes?

"They're doing what they can," responded Charles. "But they just don't know."

"People come out of comas all the time," his mother said.

He desperately wanted to tell them what he'd seen in his vision/dream, but not only could he not describe the experience accurately, he knew they'd never believe him. It was hard enough for him to believe.

He almost asked if Téa was in a coma too but stopped himself. There was no way to explain to them why he'd think she was.

"Yes, well, we can hope," his father said.

Then an idea struck him. "Can I see him?"

His father frowned and his mother sighed. "But why, Jeremy?" she asked. "We can do nothing for him. Life must go on as usual. That would be best, especially for you."

"He's my brother, Mom. I just want to see him."

His parents glanced at each other again as if they both knew something but weren't saying. They finally agreed and walked him to Leif's room.

Jeremy let the private room's door swing shut behind him and watched his brother lying so still on the bed. The blanket covered the lower half of him. He looked like he might wake up if Jeremy went over and poked him in the shoulder. Except there was an IV in his arm, and a tube attached to a plastic pouch on the floor snaked out from beneath the blanket, as if the liquid in the IV bag was being pumped in and right back out. At least he was breathing on his own.

Taking quiet steps, Jeremy went over, thought about giving him a poke, but sat in the chair by the bed instead. He gazed at his brother's face. *Where did the blond come from, and the blue eyes?*

Where had *that* thought come from?

"Who cares, Jeremy," he muttered to himself. "Genetics do what they want." He'd met his paternal grandparents, but they had both passed on now. He recalled though that they were both dark, like him, like Dad. He'd never met his mother's parents, and in the photos his mother had, they both had grey hair.

Leif's left arm, with its IV, lay on top of the blanket, while his right arm disappeared beneath the cover. Carefully, Jeremy reached over and uncovered the right arm. A band-aid had been placed over the cut on the birthmark. He placed his fingers on top of it. It was cold, as if

Leif had chunks of ice under his skin. He pulled his hand away. "Can you hear me?" he whispered. "Do you know I'm here?"

No response.

"Well, if you can hear me, you know you're a big pain in the ass most of the time, right?" Tears misted Jeremy's eyes. "But just get better anyway, okay?" He debated saying more. Should he tell him he loved him? No! That sounded too final. He wanted to believe that Leif would get better and come out of this. There had to be a way to get him out of that weird ethereal void. He rubbed his hand across his eyes, then left the room.

At the elevators, he noticed two people talking to a doctor. One of them was Téa's mother, Erla Smith. Jeremy was certain the blond man with her was Téa's father. He glanced at his parents. Neither of them seemed to notice the little group. Or had they? They seemed to be concentrating too hard on the elevators. And had Erla just glanced at them and turned quickly away? Maybe he was just imagining things. Erla worked for them; why would she ignore her employers, and they her?

"Probably a natural impulse from her brain that she had no control over," the doctor said.

Jeremy had missed the question the doctor was answering as well as the first part of the man's sentence. He'd heard enough for it to make sense though.

"But her hand moved," said Téa's mother, as if for the hundredth time. "Rose up in the air as if she was reaching for something."

"I know," said the doctor, running his hand over his face, apparently having explained it to them already. Perhaps multiple times.

So, Téa *was* in the hospital too. Why weren't his parents stopping to ask about her?

"Mom?" he said as they stepped into the elevator.

"Yes, Jeremy?"

He wanted to ask her if she'd seen them. How could she not? He wanted to ask her why Téa had the same mark on her arm that Leif did. But he couldn't find the right words, the ones to use so she'd give him a straight answer. He shook his head. "Never mind."

Chapter Eleven—Meeting the Parents

Jeremy was gone, as if he'd never materialized in the room. Téa wasn't sure he really had. His *image* had been there, but was it really him? Jeremy Noble, Leif's brother? Or was it just some shadow image of him, like the teacher and the kids in the classroom? But he had a face, while they didn't.

She *was* sure though, the paint (blood?) on her finger was real. She stared at it, trying to determine what exactly it was. Gingerly, she sniffed it.

"What are you doing?"

Téa jumped, smudging a bit of red stuff on her nose. She whirled on Leif. "What?"

He put his hands up, palms out. "Jeez, calm down. I just asked what you were doing." Then he looked at her nose and bit back a grin. She chose to ignore his grin and reached her hand out toward him. "What is that stuff?" She wiggled her fingers.

"I don't know. Paint?" He glanced at the floor, frowning.

Téa sighed. Now she had to tell him. Well, she didn't *have* to but maybe it would make things easier. Maybe this was a clue. "Look, Gate and I came down here yesterday, or sometime before, back in reality. It was dark and creepy, and there was wet red stuff on the floor."

For a moment he just stared at her. Then he grabbed her wrist, sniffed the goop on her finger, then grimaced. "Ew, Téa, that's gross."

"What is it?" She sniffed it again.

"I don't know exactly. Smells like a mix of paint and blood."

"Agreed." Grimacing herself, she wiped her hand on her pants. But it still felt dirty, so she went to the sink and turned on the faucets hoping, but not expecting, to get water. Clear water ran smoothly out of the tap. "That's weird," muttered Téa, rinsing her hands and giving her nose a wet swipe.

"What did you say?"

"I said," she replied, wiping her hands on her shirt, "that was weird."

"What is?"

"Look at this." She pointed to the water.

He put his hands on his hips. "Water coming from the tap is weird?" he scoffed.

"Leif, no one has used it in years."

"How do you know that? And why did you even bother to try using it?"

"I wanted to wash my hands. I figured there'd be a lot more air in the pipes, or there'd be rusty water. Maybe none at all. I didn't expect this. Besides, if you had been with us when we were down here before, you'd know this room, this whole basement hasn't been used since forever."

"What else did you guys see down here?"

"I didn't really stick around. It was creepy. Gate wanted to snoop around though."

"Why?"

"His parents were in some kind of cult. I don't know. I guess he thinks they might have met here or something. Atlas is his uncle, and he might have been part of it too."

"So, were our parents part of it?" Leif asked.

"Not that I know of. But, I mean, do you think they'd tell us if they were?"

"I don't know. Probably not. I guess. So, what's on that paper Jeremy tried to show you?"

"Oh!" She'd almost forgotten about that. Where did she put it? There it was, on the floor beside the blood-paint, or whatever it was. Picking it up she read, "'Cult Activity Discovered in Local High Sch ool.'"

Her gut clenched and her heartbeat sped up. Her other hand closed tightly. She gaped at Leif, who stared back, eyes wide and jaw slack. They held each other's gaze for a moment. Then Leif blew out air, as if he'd been holding his breath. "Well, what else?"

"Shearwood High, which also houses the local theatre, meeting hall, and gym has–– That's all there is. The rest is torn off. But here's part of a photo." She glanced at it, her insides starting to dance. It looked like, but no, it couldn't be, could it? She squinted, but still couldn't tell. She turned to Leif. Maybe he could make it out.

Before she could ask, he whispered, "Someone's here. I can hear them."

Téa listened, tensing. "I don't hear anything." Her voice was barely above a whisper.

"But I heard the door open or close."

Téa whirled. The door was open, had been all along. What was Leif talking about?

"Yes, I hear you," Leif yelled. "I know you're here."

Fists clenching, she dropped the clipping again. Her heart raced. Who was he talking to? "Leif, what's going on?"

"Jeremy? Hey, Jer!" Leif looked at the ceiling, the walls, all around the room. "Did you hear that? It was Jeremy. He's here."

She followed his gaze but saw nothing. This was all getting more and more bizarre. "Jeremy was here before. He's gone now," she corrected.

"No, I heard him talking to me."

"Yes, I heard him too." Tension turned to exasperation. Had he forgotten she'd also been there?

"No," insisted Leif. "This was different. Maybe he's in another room." He turned and raced out.

#

Out in the hallway, although Leif was in a hurry, he noticed that the patches of darkness between the stripes of light streaming from the classrooms had grown bigger. A glance up the hall showed fewer rooms, fewer choices. For a moment he forgot what he'd been in a rush to find. Had Téa been in one of the rooms that had disappeared? Just as quick as the thought struck, it was gone, and he knew she was here. What was that, he wondered, and how can I be so sure?

A giggle came from one of the classes. Leif remembered he'd been looking for Jeremy. He followed the sound, expecting to find Jeremy and Téa. Instead, he found a different couple, both about his age.

Dressed like the students in the other room had been, they were in each other's arms, both regarding him. The guy wore a white T-shirt with black jeans, and the girl wore a fuzzy white sweater with a blue skirt that fell in pleats almost to her ankles. Her pumps were white also.

"Come in," said the young woman, smiling. She looked familiar, but Leif was sure he didn't know her.

"Yes," agreed the young man. "It doesn't matter, everyone's welcome." He too looked familiar. Leif wondered what he meant.

"My name," said the young woman, "is Elaine Tobias. He's Charles Noble, my boyfriend." She turned in Charles's arms and pointed at something Leif couldn't see.

"These are our friends, Terry and Erla Smith." She giggled. "They were naughty and had to get married."

Leif peeked farther into the room to see the second couple. The woman with shaggy red hair wore a floral dress which did nothing to hide her pregnant belly. Her blond husband was dressed almost exactly like Charles. Except his T-shirt sleeves were rolled up, something rectangular enclosed in one sleeve. A cigarette package?

"Oh," said Elaine, "and that's our friend Roger Williams."

Behind Terry and Erla, blending in with the shadows stood another man. Who did he look——

Then suddenly her words registered with Leif, hit him hard in the gut. *Elaine Tobias. Charles Noble. Terry and Erla.*

Invisible hands tightened on his throat, cutting off his air. He froze, staring at nothing. These people were his parents as young adults. But this wasn't right. His parents hadn't met in college or high school. His mother hadn't even gone to this school. This wasn't even the right time period, was it? Had they dressed this way when his parents were young?

And the other pair, those were Téa's parents. But that couldn't be Téa in her mother's belly, could it? And why was it necessary for them to get married? Because she was pregnant? An ache began in his head. He reached up to massage his forehead.

"Are you okay?" asked Charles, stepping closer.

Elaine came with him and said, "You need to breathe."

Finally able to suck in a gulp of air, and string a few words together, Leif said, "Uh, yeah sure. I'm fine."

He slipped into a chair and pressed a finger and thumb against his eyes.

"Are you sure?" one of the girls asked. Erla, Leif thought. It didn't sound like his mother.

He nodded. What was he supposed to do now? Where was Téa? She'd figure it out in a second. Someone put a hand on his back sending a jolt of electricity down his right arm. He jumped. He and Téa seemed to be doing that a lot lately.

"Oh, I'm sorry," his mother said.

Maybe he could show her that damn mark tattooed on his body, and maybe she, or one of the others, could tell him what it meant. Would it matter? Would it change history, or the future? Would any of them even recognize it?

Taking the chance, he held out his arm. "Do any of you know what this means?"

Elaine gasped and took a step away from him. "Are you part of a cult or gang or something?"

"No."

Charles took a step toward him, peering at the red symbol. "I've never seen anything like it. Did your parents have you tattooed at birth?"

Leif scowled at him. He wanted to say *you tell me.* Instead, he shook his head. "I don't think so."

Terry and Erla crowded in behind him, peeking to see the mark.

"Your parents would tell you, wouldn't they?" asked Erla.

"It's just a birthmark," Terry told her.

Elaine frowned. "Strangely specific for a birthmark."

"What kind of people tattoo a child?" Terry spat.

Leif withdrew his arm. This was getting too weird.

"What's your name anyway?" asked Elaine.

"Leif," he replied. "Leif N–– um, Nottingham." Elaine grinned. "Like in Robin Hood?"

This time Erla giggled.

"Yeah, something like that," Leif mumbled. He stood and went to the window. The sun shone brightly. Or at least for him it did, and he wasn't about to ask the others what they saw.

The school's neatly manicured lawn spread out familiarly. The houses he could see were Hall houses. They looked the same but with brighter colours and smaller trees. Were there more of them? Had some of them been torn down? The assembly line houses had been built for military families after the war. He remembered that much from history.

Barely any vehicles travelled on the street and, he noted, no traffic lights at the turnoff to the school driveway. Had it ever actually looked like that?

"Elaine darling, you've embarrassed him. One cannot help what his name might be."

Leif put his forehead against the window, his nose centimetres from the glass. The coolness soothed his hot skin, his aching head. He didn't care about his damn name. Not now.

Where was Jeremy? He'd heard him clearly after his disappearance and now he was gone again. He looked up at the houses once more. How long ago had the war been? When had his parents attended school? He tapped his head on the window as if it might jar loose memories of things he'd forgotten about, things he never cared about before.

A touch on his other arm startled him. He straightened and saw Elaine smiling at him. "I'm sorry," she said. "I didn't mean to frighten you. And I didn't mean anything by what I said about your name. Your surname, I mean. Leif is a lovely name."

He stared, unsure what to say. For a moment, the younger version of his mother wore Téa's face. Leif blinked and it was a young Elaine again.

"It's okay," he muttered, looking away, shoving his hands into his pockets.

"I've never seen that symbol before," she whispered. "I thought maybe you were part of some tough gang or strange cult. I'm afraid of people like that." She gently placed her hand on the small of his back. He tensed.

"You needn't be so tense," Erla said, coming up on his other side. "We really won't hurt you."

Leif refused to look at either of them, especially Elaine. He didn't want to see his mother as a young babe, sometimes with Téa's face. But her voice and words were soft. In reality, his mother was tough, always in tight control.

"You don't have to be embarrassed either," Terry said. "About your name or your family."

"Yes, we can see by your clothes that you must come from an impoverished family. Can we help in some way?" asked Charles, eyeing Leif's hair and running his fingers through his own as if trying to send Leif a message.

Leif kept his hands jammed in his pockets and choked on a laugh. An impoverished family?

"Leave him alone," commanded another voice from the corner of the room, startling Leif again. He'd forgotten about the guy in the corner. "This man looks as if he carries the weight of the world on his back."

Those words were familiar. Why? Before Leif could figure it out, someone's response to Corner Guy took the attention off him. He took the opportunity to flee.

Slowing to a walk outside the room, Leif tried to make sense of it all, knowing if he went back, they would all be gone. If they really were some kind of mystic reflection of his and Téa's parents, what had happened to make his mother change so much?

And who was the baby Erla carried?

CHAPTER
Twelve—Connections

Newspaper clipping in hand, Téa headed for the stairs. Let Leif go chasing ghosts, she wanted to get to the bottom of this.

Arriving back on the first floor, she again smelled potatoes, veggies, chicken and gravy flooding the air. Her stomach made a soft rumbling sound. She wasn't hungry though, not exactly. Peckish but not starving. Even that was odd considering the amount of food she'd eaten before. In real life she'd have been in a food coma.

A peek into the kitchen showed her that the faceless cook was still there, still preparing food, although it didn't appear any more had been added to what already existed. What, or who, was this food for, she wondered. Did it mean anything or just that she was really hungry somewhere in the consciousness of her real life? "I must be in a coma too," she whispered to herself. People in comas were connected to IVs, nourishing them but not filling their bellies.

She needed answers. Now!

Maybe there *was* something useful in the library after all. Now that she had a clue, a place to start, she knew what to check on the internet, in books and magazines.

She turned to go down the hall to the library but stopped. In desperate need of a shower, she headed for the gym and the locker rooms. Halfway there, she recalled two things.

One was that Leif had warned her against going to the gym. Well, she'd stay away from there, go only to the showers. They were accessible from both inside the gym and the hallway.

The second was that if she showered, how was she going to dry off? Students were responsible for bringing their own towels if they wanted to use the showers. Would the school provide towels to the hockey team? Stupid girl, she reminded herself again. The team didn't even play here. If they were playing a home game, they played at the arena across town, not at the school.

"I'll just have to put my dirty clothes back on my clean body and let my hair drip dry," she muttered. It was better than nothing.

When she got there, she found a fluffy pink bath towel, folded and sitting on a bench. She gawked at it. Had someone forgotten it in reality, or was it just part of the vision? She poked at it. Soft and dry. Then she picked it up and gave it a delicate sniff. Smelled like laundry detergent. She shook it open, almost afraid that she'd find a familiar symbol on it. Relieved to find only the colour pink, she stripped off her clothes and laid them on the bench.

There was no soap or shampoo to be found, but just standing under the warm water, scrubbing at her skin and hair, was still refreshing. Afterwards, she padded across the room, grabbed the towel, dried off, then wrapped up her hair. She glanced at her sneakers, decided not to put them back on. Finally, she headed for the library.

The only place in the school with a skylight, the library was a large, two-story area. Reference books were here on the main floor along with periodicals, journals and other types of magazines, and computers. Most kids did everything on their phones or tablets, but the school kept computers here for the few that had little or no access to the internet. Téa couldn't imagine a library without books, even with today's technology. Some of the students, like her, preferred to hold an actual book, to smell the pages.

She headed for the cluster of computers along one wall. They appeared to be on, each one having a different screen saver. Green rolling hills on one, a beach on another, the words SHEARWOOD HIGH floating across a screen.

Wireless mice (or was that mouses?) sat beside a few of them, the others being touch screens. Jiggling the mouse next to the first computer, the image of two black-and-white-spotted puppies, both wearing big red bows, disappeared. But instead of a plain blue background, or even a fancy picture, the screen went dark except for a single bright spot in the upper left corner: a glowing white moon with the same jagged line as the one Téa had seen through the Counsellor's office window. The same as––

Icy fingers squeezed her chest, ran down her left arm. She jumped back, grabbing a chair for stability. Instead of regaining her balance, they both tumbled, and she landed on her ass. The chair thudded dully on the carpeted floor. From her position on the floor, she looked up at the screen. "What the hell?"

A white screen informed her there was NO INTERNET CONNECTION, with instructions on what to check, beneath.

"Why not?" she grumbled, scrambling to her feet. Didn't it just figure though? She grabbed the mouse again and clicked the internet icon. Nothing happened.

She tried the next computer, suspecting she'd have the same issue. She did.

Abandoning that idea, she went to the front desk where there was an old-fashioned land line and picked up the receiver. No dial tone. No connection with the outside world, the real world. Except for Jeremy on the TV.

Dropping into the big, cushioned chair behind the desk, she went over what she knew. By now she was more than convinced they were stuck in their visions, but why? How? To what end? Jeremy had said Leif was in a coma and it stood to reason she was as well. She wouldn't be here otherwise, would she?

Symbols, visions, blood, and comas. What did they all have in common? Her and Leif. But what did she and Leif have in common? Had their parents been in a cult? Were they still? Did Gate know more than he was letting on?

She'd brought the clipping with her and now looked at it again. The image was clearer, now that she had more light. It should have shocked her to her core to see what it was, but it didn't. She'd already had her suspicions. Besides, what else would it be? That symbol seemed prevalent for some reason. What did it mean?

"So, it really *is* a cult," she whispered. If she could find out more about it, maybe she could pull them out of here.

#

At the top of the stairs, Leif paused a moment. Where had Téa gone? He'd searched the basement and hadn't found her in any of the remaining rooms. Thank god he hadn't found anyone else either.

Stepping into the cafeteria kitchen, he noted it was dark and empty, the vague scent of a chicken dinner in the air.

Metal chair legs scraped on tile somewhere in the cafeteria. The hope that it was Téa surprised him. What was happening? Then he knew. Better her than some of the other things he'd seen.

He found magazines, old newspapers, and books spread out on top of one of the tables near the windows, Téa studying them (even though none were opened) and a pink towel wrapped around her head. Had she found anything out while he was getting the come-on from his own mother? He nearly gagged at the thought of young Elaine.

"Hey, you had a shower?" Where had she even found that towel?

"Oh, there you are. Finally dragged yourself up from the basement, eh?"

"Oh, ha-ha, very not funny." He knew she was kidding, but he was in no mood for it.

"Did you find what you were looking for?"

"No," he said, walking over and looking out the window beside her. The local Tim Horton's should have been visible, but all he saw were trees. Had it been like that when they'd been here before? He'd been too focused on other things that he hadn't noticed, or if he had, the thought hadn't solidified in his mind. He sighed. "How about you?"

"I've pretty much established that this belongs to a cult." She raised her left arm, indicating the mark it bore. "Now I'm just trying to find out more about it." She chose a magazine and started flipping through its pages.

He watched her a moment, debating on whether to stay here and help or go to the showers himself. What kind of help would he be? She knew things he didn't.

"I think I'll get a shower too," he said. "Where'd you get that towel?"

She looked up from her research. "It was just sitting on a bench in the girl's shower room."

"Oh." That brought back the memory of the gym, and a hesitation to go to that part of the school. Instead, he pulled out a chair opposite Téa. "You claim we're inside our visions, that this is real somehow, right?"

Without looking up she nodded. "Yeah, it has to be."

He rubbed his hands over his face. "It can't be. I just met our parents in the basement."

Finished with the magazine, she swept it closed. Eyes wide, her jaw dropped open. Then she asked, "Is that what you heard?"

"No. Maybe. I don't know. There was also another guy there by the name of Roger."

"Atlas?"

This man looks as if he carries the weight of the world on his back. Leif recalled the words, shivered violently.

"You okay?"

"No, Téa, I'm not." He rose, cold all over, and stood motionless, no idea what to do next.

"What were they doing? Our parents, I mean. How can they be here?"

A seed of anger settled in the pit of his belly, threw out a sprout of irritability. "How should I know?" His voice, high and harsh, made him even angrier, but he said nothing for a moment. He swallowed, trying to calm himself. Realistically he knew Téa wasn't responsible for this. But the thought that *she* was the one in the vision, *she* was his brother's friend, and *she* was the one looking for history books in his parents' library overrode the rationale. He reminded himself that earlier he'd wanted to protect her. From what, he still had no idea.

"Leif?"

Her voice sounded as if she were underwater. Water! God, he need-ed a shower. He ran his fingers into his limp, snarled hair. A comb would be nice right now too. That was it! He didn't care about the wonky gym.

"I'm going for a shower."

She said something, but he didn't hear what it was.

Everything was in working order in the boys' showers. He even found a blue towel hanging on a hook. It looked clean, and it occurred to Leif that if Téa had "magically" found a pink one, this one was here specifically for him anyway. The dispensers by the sinks held soap, which would have to do for now, even on his hair. Unfortunately, no clean clothes had appeared with the towel, so he'd have to wear what he had. At least his hair and skin would be clean.

Hot water streamed over him, almost literally washing away the anger. The longer he stood under the spray, the better he felt. He took a few seconds to dart out, pump soap into his hand, then back into the water. As he lathered, he focussed on the smell of the soap, the sound of the water, and the way it ran over his body, streaked with white, bubbly foam. The splatter on the tiles, gurgling in the drain. He closed his eyes, imagined himself home, in his own shower.

What seemed like only minutes later, he heard Téa's voice call to him.

"What the hell are you doing in here?" he answered. "Or are you even the real Téa?"

"Yes, it's really me," she shouted over the sound of the water. "I'm here because you've been gone a long time. I thought something might have happened."

A long time? Was she worried about him or something? "It's only been a few minutes."

"No, Leif, I don't think so. I've searched too many books and read too much stuff for it to be only a few minutes."

Had he been here that long, or were they just experiencing different things again? He looked at his fingertips. Wrinkled like raisins! Shock tingled through him. "Well, I'm fine. I'll be out in a sec."

Leif waited until the sound of her feet slapping on the tile floor faded away. He got out, grabbed the towel, and dried off. Putting on his unwashed clothes felt wrong, but then nothing about this place was right.

Back in the cafeteria, Téa had settled back at the table, everything gone except one magazine. It didn't look like one that would give her any of the information they needed. She glanced up as he walked in. "Oh," she said, surprise on her face.

"What?"

"Your hair. It has some length to it when it's not full of product."

"Yeah, so?"

"I didn't realize that before. The guy in my vision, you, had longish hair. I thought it would be Gate, because he has long hair."

"Oh. Well, too bad it wasn't him here instead of me."

She opened her mouth to speak, but he cut her off. "Finding anything in your glamour mag?" He glanced at the cover.

"Just how to apply eye makeup so the guys will notice." She rolled her eyes and tossed the magazine aside. Focussed on him.

Those eyes, Leif thought. Where else had he seen them? The basement. Everything came crashing back. Despite the refreshment of the shower, he felt filthy all over again. He sighed.

"I don't think they were our real parents," he said, picking up where they'd left off. "I mean, they were, but they were different. They were younger and everything was just wrong. My mom never even went to this school, but there she was with my dad like she belonged here. And your mom, she was pregnant.

"Pregnant? With me?" Téa frowned and started counting on her fingers.

"I don't know. I didn't ask her!" Had Téa gone insane? How could he possibly know that? He certainly had no reason to ask. Did he?

"That doesn't make sense. If Mom was pregnant with me when she was in high school, that would make me older than you."

He scratched his goatee, his rough cheeks. He wasn't quite convinced yet that they were trapped in their visions. There had to be a better, more viable option. "Well maybe they weren't actually *in* high school. I told you everything was wrong. Nothing makes any sense in this, this, wherever we are!"

"What'll it take to completely convince you?" She spread her arms out, hands wide open as if she were offering him the entire cafeteria.

He shrugged, having no idea what it would take. It both made sense, and it didn't. Where else could it be, a little voice inside asked him.

"Okay, let me explain it this way. A vision is something like a dream, right? And a dream isn't real, but it is." Téa looked a question at him to make sure he was following. Except he wasn't.

"Huh?"

"The events in a dream aren't real, but the *act* of dreaming is. Get it?"

He took a moment to process. "Okay. Yeah, I think so. But if I dream I'm eating, I don't get full; I wake up starving."

"A vision is more powerful than a dream. But I didn't really get full. I mean, my hunger went away, but for all the food I ate, I never got that overstuffed, bloated feeling."

He stared at her. How could she not have? She must have eaten more than he and Jeremy both could stuff into themselves. He glanced at his raisin-fingers again. There was that dinner smell again. Stronger this time. He sniffed. Téa smiled.

"You smell it don't you?"

He gave a brisk nod.

"My best guess is that the food is supposed to represent some kind of reality. Food is real. You cook it, you eat it. But eating in here is just an act, just symbolic."

"Of what?"

"I haven't figured that out yet. But I think we need to find out more about that cult."

"Internet?" he suggested. Why hadn't she thought of that on her own? Seemed like the logical thing to do.

She shook her head. "No connection."

"Oh. So now what?"

He lifted his hands to swoop his hair off his face, then turned them palms out to show her. "My fingers got waterlogged. How can that be? How can I have stayed under hot water that long? It never even got cold."

"I think you know the answer to that."

He lowered his hands. He did know the answer, he'd just hoped for another explanation. A chilling thought occurred to him in the silence that followed. "Téa," he said, his voice low.

Wide eyes looked back at him, roved around the cafeteria, the rest of her frozen. "What? Is there something behind me?"

"No, sorry. I just had a disturbing thought. If that baby wasn't you, do you think it might have been some sort of sacrifice for this cult our parents were in? Maybe still are in?"

Chunks of ice formed in his veins as he said it. Goosebumps appeared on his arms. Téa stared, still frozen in place. The silence in the cafeteria hissed in his ears, pressed on his shoulders. As if in slo-mo, Téa put her hands over the "O" that her mouth had formed. Somewhere a baby cried.

Then stopped.

Time swirled back to normal.

"Leif! Oh my god." Téa's voice was raspy, barely a whisper.

Shivers coursed through him as another question entered his mind. "Do you think our tattoos identify *us* as members? Is that what connects us? Why we have these visions of each other?" He couldn't raise his own voice above a whisper.

Her jaw hung open again. "Oh my, how did I not think of that?" She held out her marked arm. "They *did* have us tattooed, Leif. Their cult tattooed us!"

He struggled to get the thought into words and out of his mouth. "Wouldn't they tell us if we were members of something? Wouldn't we go to meetings or something?"

She hesitated before responding. "Well, maybe they left the cult after they got us tattooed, and now they regret it. The tattoos, I mean. Maybe it disbanded. Or maybe we have to be a certain age to join. And maybe they won't tell us because we can't know until initiation. Cults are weird that way, right?"

Her ideas only left him with more questions, one of which was, "But why doesn't Jeremy have one?"

"And why do we need blood to see each other?"

He finally went over and sat across from her. "Don't cults and blood go together like peanut butter and chocolate?"

"Okay, so-o-o," she trailed off. When she spoke again, she spoke slowly, as if thinking about each word and forming it before saying it. "Maybe the things we do here have--" She'd been slumped in the chair, but now she suddenly sat up and snapped her fingers. "The shed blood, real blood, brings on the vision. Now we're in the vision."

"So, we need to draw blood to get out?" he asked excitedly.

Téa paused again. "No, I don't think so. We never needed blood to stop it before. But maybe, well I mean, I think––"

"Why would this time be different?"

"Because," she said slowly. He could almost see the gears in her head rolling and grinding. "Because we have to do something. There's something we need to do before we can get out."

They sat staring at each other for a moment, as he digested her words, trying to put it all together. The ticking of the clock in the kitchen sounded like it was counting the seconds of his life. The smell of the food grew stronger. He glanced at the kitchen. Would he see whatever Téa had seen if he went in there? That didn't matter right now.

"Maybe it's got something to do with the kid your––*our* parents sacrificed. I mean, you know, if they really did," Leif said.

"Maybe eldest children were sacrificed and only the next child got a tattoo. That would explain why Jeremy doesn't have one. And Gate––"

"Does he have a tattoo?"

"He said he didn't. Even got me to check his back. I saw nothing."

"So much for that theory then," he said, discouraged. Gate's parents were in the cult. If he had a tattoo, everything would make a strange kind of sense. Unless Gate was lying. But why? Or did he have an older sibling no one knew about who had the mark? Before he could suggest anything, Téa's eyes went wide, and she snapped her fingers again.

"That's it!"

"What's it?"

She leapt up. "I don't need to get online for answers; I need to get on TV."

"What do you mean?"

She grinned. "Jeremy! He's our connection to the outside world. If we can contact him, we can get *him* to go online. Do some research for us." She ran across the cafeteria to the games/storage room without waiting to see if he would follow. Eventually he would, but she didn't need him to try to make a connection with his brother.

# # #

As Leif waited in the cafeteria, he went over in his head what they knew so far. Or thought they knew.

- Their parents were or had been in cults.

- Téa's mother had a child before her. A sacrifice?

- Gate's parents (and uncle, who was the school's custodian) were also in a cult. Had they sacrificed a child too? Had his parents?

- He and Téa had tattoos, but not Jeremy and not Gate, as far as they knew.

He thought of them as tattoos now, because that seemed more logical than birthmarks, despite what they'd been told. They were apparently magical too, considering what happened when they touched them. What if they touched the birthmarks again but held them longer, gave something time to happen? He stood up and drew in a deep breath. The smell of roasted chicken made his stomach growl.

Chapter Thirteen - Trying Again

Closing the door behind her, Téa glanced at the television set. Its screen was black. "Come on, Jer, I need your help." How could she get in touch with him? He had to fall asleep first. How did that even work? How could he see them in *his* dreams? What if she went to sleep? Did it work that way too? Could she find Jeremy?

If only he knew about her and Gate, then he could ask for Gate's help. But he didn't know to do that.

As she sat in one of the chairs, the door opened. Leif stepped into the room and looked at the TV, then at her. She shook her head. "He's not there. I was going to try to fall asleep to see if *I* could find *him*. Maybe I can get him and Gate to help us."

"How? Do you think Gate would help?"

She shrugged. "I think so. I don't know how, but I'm willing to try anything at this point."

"Okay." Leif held out his arm. "I was thinking, maybe we should––" He pointed to his mark. "Maybe we need to face our fears, or something like that."

"We already tried that! It didn't work. Remember?" What made him think a second shot would be different?

"But I mean for a longer time. Nobody breaks contact this time, no matter what."

Oh. That was what made him want to try a second time. She swallowed hard. While there was the possibility it might work, she was unsure of whether she was ready to try it again.

"You said you would try anything," he reminded her gently. He pushed up her sleeve. "Don't let go this time," he said, kneeling to align their arms, the symbols. "Maybe it'll get us out of here. Maybe we'll wake up."

He pressed his fingers to her mark, their tips icy. She shivered but wasn't sure if it was just from the cold. He looked at her, waiting for her to do the same. After a moment's hesitation, she slid her hand up his arm. The tingle began as soon as her fingers brushed the red skin on his inner arm. A frosty sensation spread. Their marks began to glow, then rose into 3-D. Arms melded together as if there were only one, tattoos bonding them. Blood trickled numbly from the single limb. Téa wondered if Leif felt the bonding too and resisted the urge to pull away.

"Téa," he called.

She barely heard him. The mass of flesh that had once been their arms swirled to form something that looked like a churning black hole that would suck them right in if they touched it. Where would it take them? Back home? Would they wake up? Or was it something more sinister?

Heartbeat pounding in her ears, Téa watched the twisting mass. Chills shot through her body, but she couldn't look away.

"Téa?" His voice came to her on the roar of a nonexistent wind.

She tore her gaze from the whirling blackness to meet Leif's eyes. Suddenly everything stopped. There was nothing but their breathing, that icy cold, and Leif's eyes in the moonlight.

Chapter Fourteen – Gate Gets Involved

Jeremy rubbed his eyes, trying to stay awake. The history Téa loved so much had started fascinating him as well. Shearwood's past, cults, groups, and associations that had come and gone, births and deaths. But none of it told him anything that could help him understand what was wrong with Téa and his brother. Maybe he was looking in the wrong place. Maybe he should consult some of his parents' medical books. There were some here in the library.

He sighed. Or maybe instead of fighting to stay awake, he should just let himself fall asleep, right here, right now. Leif and Téa might have learned something new, and if he dreamed that which wasn't really a dream, he could talk to them. He leaned back in his chair and closed his eyes.

How were Téa and Leif connected? Why? They were the last two he ever would have thought to have anything to do with one another. Was it because Téa's mother worked for theirs?

There wasn't a time in his memory that it hadn't been that way. He always assumed Erla had filled out an application, turned in a résumé, and went to an interview, just like any other job applicant, and that his mother hadn't even known her at that time. But what if it hadn't been that way? What if Erla and Elaine had been friends, and that was the only reason Erla got the job? He dismissed that thought. Even if they were besties, it wouldn't make any difference and wouldn't explain the birthmarks and comas.

But what if the two women were involved in something. Something illegal and/or covert? *You're losing it, Jer. That wouldn't explain things either. Would it?* His thoughts stalled, his mind drifted.

And suddenly he found himself in that dark place in the same dream he'd had before. The television set was still here, but something was wrong. At first Jeremy thought the glass had been shattered. Upon closer inspection, he saw it was still intact, but displaying a kaleido-scope effect. The faces on the screen might have been Téa's and Leif's, but they were so skewed, he couldn't tell.

The pattern changed a few times, then the screen flickered. Black-ness lasted for only a moment, then blinked into four slots, like a gambling machine. Each one flashed pictures in a blur.

As they began to slow, Jeremy could make some of them out: moons, lightning bolts, white-robed figures. And cupcakes? Slow-er still and he could make out faces. Leif's, Téa's, his own, and a red-haired girl he didn't recognize. She looked to be a bit older than Leif. The slots finally settled on those four faces, and Jeremy wondered if he'd won and what the prize was.

Shaking his head to clear his thoughts, he stared at the images. Leif's and Téa's faces were behind a broken circle symbol, kind of like the cigarette in a no smoking sign. Except part of the circle was missing and the slash, which veered off-centre a bit, was jagged like lightning. Like the birthmarks. Nothing barred the other faces. What did it all mean?

"Yeah, okay," he whispered. "Now what?"

A small, red light began to blink beside the television/slot machine, and he realized there was a lever on the side of it, as if it really were a gambling device.

He gave it a pull. The pictures spun and, when they slowed, there were four new faces. His parents and Téa's mother and father. All but his father were behind the broken circle symbol, and his father's face was fuzzy. Unlike the others who were perfectly clear. The symbol fronting his father was nearly the same, the only difference being that the circle was whole, and the jagged line ran down the exact middle.

"It's the symbol that connects them," said Jeremy, jumping at the sound of his own voice echoing in the empty space. That much was obvious. What wasn't, was the how and the why.

Téa had wanted to do research on cults. Cults usually involved symbols. Was that why they interested her so much? Because of that mark on her arm? Was she trying to find out what it meant? Was there, or had there ever been, a cult here in Shearwood? Was Téa in a coma because she learned something unexpected? From whom? And how did that involve Leif?

He pulled the lever again. And again. Each time the slots held a different combination of faces. He stopped when the same combinations started reappearing.

R-i-i-i-ng.

Jeremy jumped. What was that? He looked around. There was nothing there that could ring. Unless he really had won some sort of prize. He reached for the arm again.

R-i-i-i-i-ng.

Everything began to fade away. The ringing persisted.

His cell. He realized he was still sleeping in his home library, and his cell was ringing, waking him.

He shoved aside some books and papers to find it. A number he didn't recognize showed on the screen. Probably another one of Leif's friends looking for him. Ignoring it, he leaned back in his chair and tried to decipher what he'd seen in his dream.

# # #

The next day at school, Gate Williams approached him at lunch time. "Have you seen Téa around?" he asked quietly. "I tried calling you last night but you didn't pick up."

The unknown caller! "Oh, that was you? Sorry, I didn't recognize the number. Téa's in the hospital."

Gate's eyes went so wide Jeremy thought his eyeballs might fall out. "What happened to her? Is she okay?"

Jeremy shrugged. "No one knows what happened." He didn't bother to explain about all the weirdness surrounding the circumstances.

A frown. "What?"

"Well, she's in a coma. So's my brother. I don't really want to talk about it."

Gate scratched at his neck. Swallowed hard. He didn't say anything, but he looked guilty. Did he know something? Before Jeremy could ask, the bell rang.

"Hey, Jeremy, meet me by the office after school, okay?" Gate called, heading down the hall.

"Ah yeah, sure." Whatever that was all about.

After the final bell had rung, Jeremy made his way back to his locker. He stood fiddling with his books, pretending to be busy while he debated whether or not he should meet Gate. Why had Gate called to ask about Téa? He and Gate weren't friends and, as far as he knew, Téa wasn't friends with him either. For that matter, how had Gate even gotten his cell number? He supposed Gate could have simply observed who his friends were, then asked one of them for it.

Jeremy recalled the other day on the front steps of the school. Téa had teased him about scaring Gate away. What had he been doing there? What had he even wanted? But what if Gate knew something that could help her and Leif? Jeremy had no clue what the guy could possibly know, but it was worth taking a chance.

"Jeremy?"

Startled from his thoughts, he dropped the book he was holding. It happened to be one about cults. He snatched it up before whoever called his name could see it. He was aware of someone giggling, but the voice had already told him his visitor was female. He straightened, holding the book against his chest.

Kim! Wasn't that the girl Leif had a crush on? Were they dating?

Kim giggled. "Oh god, Jeremy, I'm sorry. I didn't mean to scare you."

He nodded, accepting her apology, his face heating up. "Uh, yeah, sure. It's fine."

"I heard that Leif was in the hospital. Is that true?"

"Yes."

"What happened? Was he in an accident or something?"

"He's in a coma," Jeremy said.

"Oh! He didn't, did he try . . . I mean, I heard that . . . someone told me he committed, tried to commit suicide."

Jeremy stared at her. Who on Earth had said that?

"No, no, no. Not at all." Jeremy thought of the cut on his arm. He *had* cut himself, but it certainly wasn't suicide. People didn't cut the insides of their elbows to kill themselves, and that wouldn't have caused a coma anyway. He took a deep breath and wondered, not for the first time, if Téa had any cuts on her arm or anywhere else.

"Are you okay?" asked Kim.

He nodded again.

"I'm sorry, this must be difficult for you."

"The doctors don't know what's wrong. That's the worst part."

"Um, I heard Gate Williams telling someone that Téa Smith was in there too. Is that true?"

"It is."

"Oh. Okay, well, were they together? I mean, not like dating, but when it happened?"

"Gate and Téa?"

"No, I meant Téa and Leif."

"No, Leif was home. I don't know where Téa was, but probably home too." He'd never thought about it that way, but where else would she have been? The whole town probably would have heard about it if it had happened at a public place.

She blinked in surprise. "That's kind of weird, isn't it?"

You don't know the half of how weird it is, thought Jeremy. "Yeah, it is."

"I'm sorry," she repeated. "I just wanted to hear it from someone who would know what was really going on. Hope they get better soon."

"Yeah, thanks."

She smiled then turned and walked away, her heels clacking on the floor. Jeremy watched her for a minute, then headed for the office.

Gate was already waiting for him.

"Téa was interested in cults," Gate started before Jeremy could say a word, before any kind of greeting. "I don't know why she wanted to go to the basement, but I knew about the elevator, so I took her there. I mean, you knew she was into cults, right?"

Into cults?

"She was doing a school project on cults," Jeremy corrected.

Gate chuckled. "Well, yeah, that's what I meant. I think that's why she wanted to go to the basement. After you told me she was in the hospital, I got thinking about it. I want to show you something."

Jeremy didn't know Gate very well, but knew he was shy and quiet. That might explain why he'd backed off when Jeremy approached Téa, but it sure didn't explain this chatterbox now. He was just as bad as Téa when she got wound up talking about Shearwood's history. Maybe the two of them were better friends than he realized. It seemed they had a common interest.

Gate led Jeremy into Atlas's office, where he showed him an elevator that he said went down to the basement.

"Come on." He beckoned, pressing a button that called the elevator, even though the spray paint on the doors claimed it was out of service.

As Jeremy joined Gate, he wondered when his school had gotten so weird.

The basement was dark with only emergency lights creating spooky shadows in the hall. Gate sniffed. "Do you smell anything?"

Jeremy smelled the air. "Damp, musty basement."

"Yeah," Gate said slowly, turning to give Jeremy a look that asked if there was something wrong with him.

"What?"

"Uh, never mind." Gate shook his head.

What was that about? wondered Jeremy. Gate was one weird guy.

He led Jeremy to a room that was empty except for a white pedestal sink and a wooden wall cabinet with moon carvings on its sides, old spice bottles on its shelves. No, this couldn't be the same place, could it? The bottles in the room in his dream had been full. Even if, somehow, it *was* the same room, what could it possibly mean?

"We came in here, and there was wet paint on the floor. *She* thought it was blood."

"She didn't tell me about this," Jeremy told him, wondering if Téa had told Gate anything about her birthmark.

Gate didn't respond to Jeremy. He turned on his cell phone torch and shone it on the floor. "I wanted to check out the other rooms. But she was afraid to. It's gone!"

"What's gone?"

Gate looked at him, his face in the narrow beam, his eyes behind his glasses shadowy and creepy. "The paint. Or blood. Whatever it was is gone."

"So, someone cleaned it up. That's a no-brainer. Duh!"

"No one ever comes down here though."

"Obviously someone did. Isn't that why there's an elevator in Atlas's office?"

Gate looked at him as if that hadn't occurred to him. "Well, Roger comes down here to store things sometimes. But I think he's the only one."

"Who's Roger?"

Rolling his eyes, Gate looked exasperated. "Atlas. That's his real name."

"Oh. Maybe he cleaned it up then."

"Okay, sure. Maybe. But why was there wet paint here in the first place? Jeremy, you're telling me Téa is in a coma. After she touched it. There has to be a connection!"

Jeremy took a moment to take in what Gate was suggesting. It was troubling, and his first thought was to tell someone like the principal. But that didn't explain Leif. "So, I take it you didn't touch it."

"Yeah, I did. But I don't have any marks anywhere on my body."

So, she had told him about the birthmark.

"What else did she tell you?"

Gate narrowed his eyes at Jeremy. "What do you mean? Is there something else she should have told me?"

Jeremy thought quick. "No, I just wondered if there was some way to help them."

"I don't think we can do that. If coma patients could be helped out of them, don't you think it would be common knowledge?"

"Well," Jeremy began, then changed his mind. Why had Gate even brought him down here? It seemed more like he wanted to show Jeremy something that was no longer there, than it did that he wanted to help Téa.

"Do you think someone is trying to hide something?" asked Gate, either not hearing Jeremy's hesitation or ignoring it.

"Like what?" Jeremy leaned closer to Gate and whispered. "You mean like some kind of cult ritual or something?"

Gage jumped back as though Jeremy had slapped him. "Cult?"

This whole situation was getting weirder by the minute. Jeremy shrugged and opened his mouth, but no words came out.

"Wait a sec!" Gate grabbed Jeremy's arm. "Is *she* in a cult? Is that what that mark on her arm is?"

Pulling out of Gate's grasp, Jeremy found his words. "No. Calm down. You were the one that suggested someone might be trying to hide something."

"I was guessing. You suggested cults."

"Gate, what if that stuff you guys found on the floor is gone because the cult is still around, and some member cleaned it up after you saw it."

Brows knitted together in a frown, Gate said, "Do you think someone hurt Téa because she saw it?"

"If they did, you might be in trouble too."

Gate didn't even flinch. Just shook his head. "No, that doesn't make sense. If that was the case, I'd be in a coma, not your brother."

"We need to talk to them."

"Who?"

"Leif and Téa."

"How?"

"I can see them when I go to sleep."

"You can? That's weird, isn't it? Do you have one of those funny marks too?"

"Nope!"

Chapter Fifteen—The Creature

It was hard to say when they broke apart, or even if they had. Although it appeared they were separated, Téa could still feel Leif's touch. Her arm had stopped tingling, and the tattoo had stopped glowing, but now there was a voice in her head that wasn't hers. She couldn't be sure it belonged to Leif, either.

Glancing at him, Téa started to speak but paused as she noticed movement from the corner of her eye. Turning toward the cafeteria, she saw the hooded, faceless thing from the kitchen approaching them. Moving among the tables and chairs, it slipped around them, yet somehow through them at the same time.

The smell of roast chicken, bacon, and pumpkin pie wafted in the air, gently at first, then so strong it made Téa want to throw up.

She glanced at Leif again. Staring wide-eyed at the creature, Leif took a blind step toward her. Back to the creature, closer now. It pushed the hood off its head. Unable to look away, Téa opened her mouth to scream. But what she saw wasn't scream-worthy. A simple human male, maybe Leif's age. Big brown eyes and orange-brown hair that curled down to his shoulders.

He reached his hands out to them. "I have the answers you seek. Come with me."

# # #

The smell of a roast-chicken dinner filled Leif's nostrils. He'd never smelled anything in his dreams before. But this wasn't really a dream, was it? He tried to recall what Téa had said about visions when he noticed her watching him, about to say something. Instead, she turned away. Leif turned to see what had drawn her attention.

Something wearing a robe and without a visible face made its way toward them. Was that what Téa had seen in the kitchen? Leif stepped toward her.

As the thing neared them, moving around chairs, through them, it pulled off its hood. Leif didn't think he'd ever seen anything scarier looking. He couldn't even tell if it was male, female, a combination of both, or neither. But it appeared to be older than time itself, wrinkles upon wrinkles sagging over its face. The eyes, deep black craters, peered out between folds of grey, scabby skin. Tufts of hair puffed out from its cheeks and chin. Brown spots covered its bald head. Lips caved into its mouth as if it had no teeth. A bulbous nose dominated its face, drooping toward its chin as if it were melting. It reached its hands out to them. "I have the answers you seek. Come with me."

Téa lifted her own hand to the creature's hand. "Téa, don't," Leif cried.

She didn't acknowledge him. The mark on her arm glowed again as she reached for the gnarled, wrinkled hand.

It was then that Leif noticed the creature had the same mark. Although the long white sleeve of its robe covered it, Leif could see it glowing through the cloth.

Its black eyes glittered. The sunken mouth seemed to mock him. It knew he was afraid, knew there was nothing Leif could do to save Téa if it grabbed her. She (they) might even die. Her fingers entwined with the creature's. Why did it want her, anyway?

With no time to figure it out, Leif hurled himself at Téa, knocking her to the floor and pulling her hand out of the thing's grasp. She grunted beneath his weight. Twisting his head around, he saw the look of shock on the ugly face just before it quivered, then shimmered out of sight.

Téa squirmed beneath him, then beat her fists against his chest and shoulders. Around them, the room darkened. Tables and chairs blinked out as if each were a light and someone was turning them off, one by one. Leif pushed himself up. Téa jumped to her feet and, still yammering, she grabbed his arm.

"What?" he asked, ignoring her grasp, watching each window blink out. Even the smells were fading.

"Are you deaf? I said, 'What did you do that for?' You hurt my arm!"

"Didn't feel a thing," he muttered, then turned to look at her. Glaring at him, she rubbed her arm. About to tell her it was probably the creature that hurt her, he instead gave a start. Not because of her stare, but because she appeared caught in a spotlight. Her long brown hair shone as it hung over her shoulders, and her golden-brown eyes sparkled. She was beautiful. But not in a hot girl sort of way. More like maybe a cousin.

"What's wrong with you?" she demanded.

He blinked. "Don't you see?" he asked, swinging his arm in an arc.

She looked around, confused. "See what? He's gone, you scared him away."

"He who?" How could she tell it was a male in the dark?

She shook her head as if he were stupid. "Never mind. Why'd you tackle me?"

Tackle her? "I was saving your life. How could you not know that? That thing was evil. Don't you see the darkness around us now?"

"What are you talking about?"

Then Leif understood. It was happening again. They weren't seeing the same things. What had she seen, that she was so willing to go with, instead of the scary-ass, ugly creature he'd seen? What was she seeing now?

"I don't know what you saw, but the creature I saw looked faceless until it took off its hood. The face it did have was ugly and horrible and terrifying. And now, it just keeps getting darker and darker in here."

"Dark?" Téa asked, calmer now. Then she gasped.

Leif felt the floor shift beneath them. "You feel that?"

She nodded and looked down.

The smell of cool, damp air and wet earth rose up. The floor beneath Leif's bare feet felt like ice. He looked down. At first he couldn't see anything through the darkness. Soon, gray concrete became visible. He frowned. Then he saw it.

#

The sudden tilt gave Téa the sensation of being on a ferry. But this wasn't the deck of a boat. It was the basement.

Suddenly Leif cried out, "Téa, do you see that?"

She did. Red markings, like paint, or maybe blood, appeared on the floor. Hesitantly, she knelt and touched it. It was wet, like she knew it would be.

"It's the symbol. Our tattoo. But where are we?" Leif's head swivelled madly, his gaze darting everywhere.

Turning to take in her surroundings, she saw a small, dirty, rectangular window on one side. Red-tinged moonlight shone in through it. The wooden cabinet with the moons carved into it was there and so was the sink. She moved to peer into it. Candles and the sodden remains of old cake lay inside.

Her heart throbbed in her throat, and her belly quivered as she turned to Leif. At the same time, he turned to her. "The school basement," they said as one.

#

A buzz of electricity shot up Leif's leg. He looked at the floor and found that he'd stepped on the painted mark. At least he hoped it was paint. When he removed his foot, the tingle stopped. He knelt to touch it. Wet, sticky liquid covered his right hand. A current flowed through his fingers and trickled up to the matching symbol on his arm. Strangely, he felt nothing in his left hand, even when he touched it.

"What are you doing?"

"Come and try this. It doesn't hurt. It's like sticking your tongue on a 9V battery."

She knelt again. "Leif, it's wet paint. Or blood."

He grimaced but said, "Yes, I know. But neither paint nor blood does this. Touch it."

"I did. Nothing happened."

"Oh." Maybe it was just him, maybe he had a lot of natural electricity in his body. He knew some people who couldn't wear digital watches because of the natural electrical current in their bodies. Or maybe she'd used the wrong hand.

"Which hand did you use?"

She raised her right arm. "Why?"

"Your mark is on the left, correct? Use that hand."

She hesitated, but finally touched it.

The moment her fingers made contact, she jumped to her feet and pulled her hand away, eyes wide. But he knew. She'd felt it too.

Then the room began to grow dark again. Funny, Leif thought, he couldn't remember it getting lighter. The moon still gleamed through the window, but as a mist rose up around them, the beam seemed to narrow. Was that why it was getting darker? Leif wondered.

Deep, droning voices chanted or sung, from somewhere in the distance. They grew closer and closer until it sounded like they were right outside the room. The door banged open, and Leif leapt to his feet.

"They are both here, Vainquir," a strange voice said. "Are we to use them both?"

"Silence," another voice roared. "The girl is important too."

Leif searched for the source of the voices, but he saw nothing.

"Keep them in the Circle of Moonlight," commanded the second voice.

Téa gasped. Leif reached out and pulled her toward him. His heart pounded against his ribs, and his head pulsed with thoughts he didn't understand. As she pressed her back against his chest, he became aware of his love for her, his need to protect her. He'd felt it before, back at the school, but it was much stronger now.

"Let go of the girl." It was still the second voice, harsh and bellowing.

"No, I won't let you take her." His arms pinned her to him. Why did they want her? What were they going to do?

Chapter Sixteen-Familiarity

The woman sitting on the other side of Téa's bed looked vaguely familiar, but Jeremy couldn't figure out why. She'd been introduced to him as Darla Smith, Téa's aunt, but he had never met her before. Blue eyed, with short-cropped red hair, she looked to be a little older than Leif. "What did the doctors mean when they said they'd gone further into the comas?" Jeremy asked.

Darla startled at the sound of his voice, then relaxed. She shook her head. "I don't know." Stroking Téa's cheek, she continued, "You know, it was her drinking that put you in here."

Whose drinking? wondered Jeremy. Did Téa have a problem that he didn't know about? No, Darla had said *her* drinking, not *your* drinking.

As if she had heard his thoughts, Darla explained. "My sister and her husband. Téa's parents. They always fought. About everything, but mostly about Erla's drinking. She's an alcoholic." Suddenly she looked up, somewhat alarmed. "You did know about that, didn't you?"

Jeremy nodded, and he wondered, not for the first time, if his parents knew. He'd never worked up the nerve to ask.

"Maybe if they'd paid more attention to Téa, she wouldn't be here."

Jeremy understood that Darla was worried about her niece, but he knew there was no connection between her and Erla's drinking. He wondered how Darla was connecting it. What did she think happened?

"What happened to your brother?" asked Darla. "He's in here too, isn't he?"

Again, Jeremy nodded. "Yeah, but no one knows what's wrong. It just sort of happened. My parents found him collapsed on the floor." Or maybe they'd found him in his bed. The morning it had happened was all a blur.

Darla had told him earlier that Erla found Téa the same way, on the floor. But where was Erla now? Off drinking while her daughter lay comatose in the hospital? Where was Terry? He thought about asking, but it wasn't his business, nor would it change things. Still, the thought made him angry.

"Do your parents have a drinking problem too?" She paused, then said, "I'm sorry. That's a personal question."

"It's fine. They don't."

As Darla kept fussing over Téa, Jeremy caught sight of Téa's left arm. It was the first time her arm had been outside the blanket since she'd come to the hospital a week ago. He noticed there wasn't a cut across it, like there had been on Leif's. Was it really a cult mark? Had she and Leif been marked *for* something? Like maybe a sacrifice? That idea had been Gate's. Both he and Jeremy were anxious to speak to Leif and Téa again, but he hadn't been able to find them. Was that because they'd gone deeper into their comas, as the doctor had said?

"What's this?" he blurted, pointing to the circular mark, to avoid thinking about what it could mean. Darla didn't seem concerned about him seeing it, but maybe she knew something about it.

"A birthmark."

"It looks like a symbol of some sort. Do you have one?"

Darla looked at him, frowning. He supposed she was wondering what business that was of his. He was about to apologize for asking when she simply said, "No."

"I don't either."

"So?"

"Well, Leif has one too."

"You mean a birthmark?"

Jeremy nodded. "Yes, it's exactly the same as hers, only on his right arm, not his left. I touched them both at the same time once and got a shock. Like when you stick your tongue on a battery."

That got her attention. Her eyes widened. "What do you mean? How can a birthmark do that?"

"I don't know. That's why I thought maybe it was a symbol of some sort."

Darla looked at Téa's arm, traced the mark with her finger. "I'm sure what you did has nothing to with their condition."

Jeremy had never considered that. Now that he did, he quickly dismissed it. If he'd caused it, it would have happened at that time, not later. "There was something else," he said. "Leif had a cut on his arm. Across the mark."

Darla cocked her head at him. "Téa had a cut on her finger. But I don't know what that would have to do with anything. Apparently, she'd just been cleaning up some broken glass."

"But they both have those marks, they both had cuts, and now they're both in comas. What does it mean? How are they connected?"

Darla sighed. "I'm sorry. Other than your parents, I don't think there's any connection. But that's really weird, isn't it?"

"Yeah. Um, her parents weren't in any kind of cult that might have required a tattoo, were they?" Jeremy squirmed in his chair, his face hot.

Darla only laughed. "Erla and Terry? Can you imagine those two in a cult? The leader would kick them out after dealing with them for just a couple of days. Besides, neither of them has a tattoo or birthmark. Not that I'm aware of."

Jeremy just smiled and nodded. So much for that idea.

The cell phone in Darla's hand buzzed. She glanced at the phone, then at her niece. "I'm sorry, Téa, but I've got to get to work. I'll come by again later. Love ya, kid."

Pulling on her jacket, she stood and smiled at Jeremy. "Do you think she can hear me?"

"Yes, I do." He wondered if Darla went to sleep, would she see Téa the way he did.

"So do I." She headed for the door. Jeremy followed her. Maybe he'd grab something to eat, then find a nice quiet place to curl up and go to sleep.

Chapter Seventeen – Thoth

Téa clung to Leif as if she never wanted to let go. The last place she'd ever imagined she'd want to be was in Leif's arms, but now that she was, the scent of him comforted her. She felt protected.

The voices had silenced, and the ray of moonlight focussed solely on the two of them. Darkness embraced the beam.

"What's happening?" Téa asked so softly that Leif had to lower his face closer to hers, his rough cheek scratching across her smooth one. "What did you say?"

She repeated her question.

"I wish I knew."

Within her circle of safety, she peered into the dark but could see nothing. The air around them changed. From the damp chill of the basement to the crisp cool of a late autumn afternoon. From the dank musty smell to the earthy scent of wet, rotting leaves.

Gradually the darkness began to lift, as though morning was coming to chase away the night. Téa could now make out the shapes of leafless trees, but little else. Soon the mist lifted from the grass, revealing that they stood in a field next to a forest, the evergreens behind oaks and maples identifiable now, but nothing looked familiar.

A hooded figure stepped out from behind a tree. Leif's grip on her tightened, but Téa was neither surprised nor frightened by the appearance. It was as if she knew it had accompanied them from the basement. That knowledge astounded her more than the figure itself had.

"Where are we?" Leif demanded.

The creature reached up with a gloved hand and pushed its hood down to reveal a man's face. Long, wavy orange-brown hair and brown eyes. The guy from the cafeteria! "You are in Demon's Field."

Demon's Field? Téa pulled gently away from Leif. At first, he held firm, but she persisted, and he let her go. She took in more of the view as the day brightened, turning and craning her neck to see as much as she could. She had read something about Demon's Field. It was in or near Shearwood hundreds of years ago.

Men, women, and children dressed in animal skins moved among domed sweat lodges, longhouses, and birchbark tipis, apparently going about daily chores. In the distance, a tall grey castle rose as if from the clouds. A castle? "I think the question is not *where* we are, but *when* we are," she said.

"It is the year of Our Lord thirteen hundred and one," responded the man.

It was 1301! Téa looked at him again. His clothing suggested he might have been from the fourteenth century, but she couldn't be sure. She could see his leggings and simple leather shoes, but his cloak covered the rest.

"But where is Demon's Field?" inquired Leif, also looking around. Téa wondered if this time he saw the same things she did.

"Epjilasi," of course," said the man.

So, she'd been correct. But this couldn't be Epjilasi. Castles never existed in Epjilasi. Not in 1301, or ever.

"Where?" asked Leif.

"Ep-chi-*lah*-si," said Téa slowly, pronouncing each syllable for him. "It's the historical name for Shearwood."

"I guess I should have listened more in History class," Leif muttered. "But why did they change it, and what does that word mean?"

"I'm pretty sure it means 'welcome'," she said as she continued looking around. If this was Epjilasi or Shearwood, she should've been able to see the river. They were on top of a hill, after all, and the river had always been there. "When the Europeans first came over, the Native people used that word. The Europeans thought it was the name of the place and called it that for a while."

She took a few steps and saw it, as grey as the horizon. The Commerce River at the bottom of the hill, its other bank shrouded in the fog. Even without the bridges, houses, and buildings, Téa knew it was the same river that cut through her hometown. Then she remembered about Demon's Field. She whirled around to face Leif. "Demon's Field is where they built Shearwood High, right?"

"You're the history buff."

"You know your history well," said the cloaked male, affirming that she was correct. He smiled. "Please, She-that-has-no-name, tell us more."

"Hey, wait! What did you call her?" asked Leif.

"She-that-has-no-name, of course. You are Thoth, and I am Sen."

Sen? Wasn't that the name of a Lunar god? Téa wasn't sure, and she didn't want to ask.

"Thoth? My name's——"

Sen held up his hand to stop whatever Leif was going to tell him and nodded at Téa. "Tell me what else you know."

"In the fourteenth century, only the Native Americans lived here. Epjilasi was renamed Shearwood later. Actually, Sherwood, but it got spelled wrong. The settlers had made their homes here, near the river." She glanced at the castle. Did that represent the Europeans? "It was never a peaceful settling though. The Europeans and Natives fought skirmishes in which many on both sides were killed. Many diplomatic groups were formed, each trying to bring peace to the nation."

She stopped. There was no more for her to tell. Or rather, there was plenty she could tell, but nothing that seemed pertinent to what Sen was asking. She looked at Leif. He stood there with a dumb grin on his face as though he was proud of her. Again, she wondered, but didn't ask, *What's happening?*

"Very good," said Sen.

"Why is any of that important?" asked Téa. "What I know about Shearwood doesn't matter. Tell me something I don't know."

"What you don't know is what has never been written."

"How can she know what hasn't been written?" cried Leif. "That's stupid!"

But Sen paid him no attention as he prattled on. "It is said that the mists of Demon's Field dance in the moonlight, and anyone caught in the dance will gain strength from the moon herself. I have heard that children conceived during the moon dance will have the gift of visions."

Téa and Leif glanced at each other. What on Earth did that mean, conceived during the moon dance? Had both their parents made love under the moonlight? Yeah, thought Téa, probably in the backseat of Terry's second-hand, rusted-out car. Charles and Elaine were probably a little more "romantic," at least doing it in the back of a half-ton truck on a blanket.

Suddenly Sen shouted, "Sin has broken the circle; now you must make it right."

Téa jumped at the sudden volume and stumbled backward, falling onto the grass. Then Sen was gone. Leif came to help her up.

"Leif, what's happening here?" she asked for the third time, not expecting an answer. Leif didn't know any more than she did. But she needed to ask, desiring answers which weren't forthcoming.

Fear wound icy fingers inside her. Her own fingers curled into tight fists at her side. And there were the tears! A single tear from each eye slid slowly down her cheeks. How long had it been since she'd shed them?

Leif lifted his arm to study his tattoo. He pointed to the broken circle. "Is this the circle he meant? It's broken, right?"

Téa's only response was to press her face against his chest. *Dammit, Téa, what's the matter with you?*

He wrapped her in a hug.

"I don't know," she choked out after a minute or two, when the tears stopped.

A few minutes more and she pulled away. "But if it is, who broke it, and why do *we* have to fix it?"

"Huh? What are you talking about?"

Téa giggled a little. Maybe he hadn't changed that much. "Answering your question from before. About the broken circle."

"Oh that." He chuckled. "It has to be our parents, doesn't it?"

"Why?" But even as the question came out of her mouth, she knew he had to be right.

"Remember I told you I saw them back in the school?" he said.

"So, they broke the circle? How?"

"I don't know how, but maybe that's why they were there. Plus, the baby, remember?"

"You said Atlas was there too. What does he have to do with it, other than being in the same cult?"

"I said I thought it looked like him. But I think his name was Roger."

"That's Atlas's real name. Gate said his mom dated Atlas first."

Leif scratched at his chin and tugged his scraggly beard hairs. "What does any of this have to do with anything? Is the cult the connection?"

"It has to be. Other than that, I have no clue. Sen wasn't very helpful."

They both were silent for a moment as they searched their surroundings for clues, something that would help them figure this all out.

Moon dances and children with visions. Obviously, those children were her and Leif. Sen had said something wasn't written, and then what about the Europeans and the Indigenous peoples? An idea began forming.

"Diplomatic groups tried to bring peace," she muttered. Peace. War. Why were wars fought? Treason? Deception? Betrayal? Were any of those things the sin that broke whatever circle had been broken? She pushed up her sleeve to glance at her arm. Did the dot represent the moon? Or was the dot a blemish on the moon?

"So, we're like, children of the moon?" asked Leif. He held his arm out next to hers. "Is that what these tattoos are for? Are *we* members of this cult after all?"

"Maybe they mark *us* as sacrifices. It explains why Jeremy and Gate don't have any."

"But why us? What was Sen talking about?"

Téa dropped her arm back down to her side. "Our parents must have done something, Leif. The four of them. Together." Shivers crawled down Téa's spine. It all seemed so interesting before, now it was just creepy. "I have no idea how they chose us." She searched her brain for something that made sense, but there was nothing. Leif was firstborn, but, apparently, she wasn't. Why did she need to be sacrificed if her parents had already made one? Had Leif's parents done the same?

"He called you 'She-that-has-no-name,' and me 'Thoth.' Are those some kind of weird moon names?"

"Thoth is––"

"Téa!" A voice boomed from everywhere at once.

She jumped, grabbed Leif's hand, and searched desperately until she finally saw Jeremy's face shimmering in the sky. Without taking her eyes off him, she finished.

"Thoth is the Egyptian god of the Moon."

Chapter Eighteen—Vainquir

Leif didn't understand his growing need to protect Téa. Though it seemed bizarre, it felt more natural than most anything he'd ever done. He reached for her when he heard the booming voice call to her, but let his arms fall back to his sides when he realized it was only Jeremy.

"Hey, Jer, what's up?" asked Téa as if they were meeting each other in the school hallway. "Where are you?"

Jeremy looked sheepish. "In the cafeteria at the hospital."

"How long," asked Leif, "have we been in comas?"

"A week. Why? What's it seem to you?"

A week? Leif wasn't sure how long it seemed to him. He and Téa just kept going, on to the next thing as if there were no days or nights. They hadn't slept, they'd barely eaten, and he wasn't tired or hungry. "A day, maybe. It's hard to tell here."

"Where's here?" asked Jeremy.

"It keeps changing," Leif told him.

"We're inside our visions," said Téa. "And everything is messed up."

"Visions? What are you talking about?" Confusion registered on Jeremy's face.

Leif had never told anyone about the visions, not even Jeremy. Apparently, Téa hadn't mentioned it either.

"I'll explain later," replied Téa. "Right now, I need you to talk to Gate."

"I have. He took me to the basement and showed me where the paint had been. He said you touched it, and he thinks that's why you're in a coma. But that can't be it. Leif didn't touch it, did he? I mean, you weren't even together, were you?"

"No to both questions," said Téa. "And it's not paint. It's blood. I don't know what it means, Jer."

Chanting began somewhere in the forest. Jeremy's face began to glow blue white like the moon. "Jeremy," Téa called out. "Ask Gate who 'Sen' is. And 'Morgan'."

Morgan? Who was Morgan, and why was she asking about them? Wondered Leif.

Blue-grey mist came up from the ground to encircle them. Jeremy's face flickered. "What? I can't hear you. Someone's trying to wake me up. Did you say Morgan?"

Robed, hooded beings emerged from the forest bathed in the blue-white glow from Jeremy's moon face.

"Yes. My dad calls Mom that sometimes. Jeremy! Don't wake up," cried Téa, moving closer. "He said we could gain strength from the moon."

Jeremy's face flickered again. "Who? Téa, it's getting hard to hear you. I can't hold onto my dream."

Téa reached for her friend. "Take my hand!"

Jeremy's hand came into view, big as the moon and bathed in the blue-white light, giving it an eerie glow. It reached for hers, then flickered. "I can't!"

The beings were nearly halfway across the field now. Jeremy flickered, his hand pulled back. Then he was gone leaving them in blackness. The chanting stopped. The grass rustled, then stilled. Leif wrapped both arms around Téa.

"They have stolen the moon, Vainquir," came a voice that sounded like Sen's.

"No. The moon is innocent," a man's voice spoke. "She is always innocent."

The moon is innocent, thought Leif. What did that mean? And what did it have to do with the moon being stolen? Téa's back pressed into his chest; her hands slipped over his arms.

A flame blazed in the dark, revealing a white-robed figure, face obscure inside a hood. He held a thick, twisted stick in one hand, the end of which burned bright slightly higher than his head. "My children, it is time for the truth to be revealed to you."

He stepped into the misty circle. Several other robed, hooded figures gathered behind him in the shadows outside the circle. He thrust the stick into the ground, then pushed his hood back to reveal the face of a man with long grey hair. His features, although distorted in the flame light, were nothing out of the ordinary except for one thing.

A mark on his cheek glowed, much like the mist. An unbroken circle, split down the middle with a jagged line, a solid circle angled above it. The same as the symbol in the newspaper, nearly the same as the tattoos on their arms.

"What do you want?" Leif cried. "I won't let you take her."

The man only smiled. "Wonderful. I don't want to take her from you, Thoth. I never wanted to take her from you. I am pleased to hear you say these things to protect her. It's how it should be."

He stepped toward them and held out his hand, a hand that looked no different from Leif's own. Older perhaps, but still with four fingers and a thumb. "I am Vainquir and it is time to know the truth."

"What do you want? Who is Thoth?"

Vainquir dropped the proffered hand, ignoring the questions. "Show me your birth symbols."

Their marks were already glowing; there was no hiding them. Leif held out his right arm, Téa her left. Vainquir placed a hand over each one, covering the entire symbol. Electricity flowed through them, and for a moment it seemed as if they were all a single being.

Images flashed through Leif's mind: His parents, Téa's, Jeremy, people he didn't know. Hundreds of faces, thousands. The flame on the stick behind Vainquir flickered and blazed as though it couldn't decide whether to die out or burn brightly. Vainquir chanted softly. Leif couldn't make out most of the words, but "Mother Moon" seemed prominent among them.

The flame finally burned out and the moon (the real moon, not his brother's face) shone too bright in the sky. A stream of moonlight, like a flashlight beam, trailed to the ground, illuminating the robed beings behind Vainquir. One by one they disappeared until only six remained. Three of the six were in white hooded robes. Three wore red robes, their heads bare of any hood. Two were clearly pregnant. All their faces were obscured to him, almost like the privacy blur in videos. They could have been anybody.

Chapter Nineteen-Truth

A bolt of lightning flashed, and suddenly Leif and Téa were on the outside, looking into a three-walled room. The robed men and women stood around a painted symbol on the floor. A white ceramic sink stood beneath a window, and a cabinet carved with moon shapes hung on one wall. The room in the school basement! So, the cult did meet there! Téa's fingers curled as she started to cry out. But as she did, the flame on Vainquir's crude sceptre blazed high. Leif took her hand in his.

"Silence!" the ancient man demanded.

Nails digging into the palm of one hand, fingers on the other steel-clamped around Leif's, Téa pressed tighter against him. Both their bodies were stiff with unease.

One of the women with a baby bump took a child from a third figure, the blur easing to reveal a glimpse of her face.

"Mom?" Leif muttered under his breath.

Looking at the toddler's arm, she cried out, frightening the child. She covered the blond curls with her hand and pressed the baby's head gently to her shoulder, trying to soothe the sobs. Chubby baby arms went around her neck.

"I have been around for hundreds of years," Vainquir said. "I founded the Motherhood of the Moon, and my people and I have been worshipping her ever since."

"It is a cult," whispered Téa, hoping Vainquir didn't hear. "Some sort of Moon cult."

Either he didn't or he chose to ignore her as he continued to speak.

"Under my rules, no one is to have any secrets." He directed these words to the group of four, the other two remaining in the background. "You knew this when you joined me and my Trusted Ones.

"Under my rules, no one is to betray their bonded ones, the one they committed themselves to for life. If you wished to break the bond, you should have come to me first.

"Koon, do you wish to stay by Myst's side, or do you choose for the bond to be broken?"

The distortion lifted on the figure Koon's face.

"Dad!" Leif's muscles tensed even more, if that were possible. His grip on Téa tightened. She winced, both from the pressure and the outcry, and waited for him to be reprimanded. None came this time.

Charles Noble, the one called Koon, looked at Elaine, the one called Myst. "Thoth is not my child?" His voice sounded broken, full of tears.

Myst dipped her head, giving a slight shake.

Vainquir whipped around and, grabbing the stick he'd earlier planted in the ground, gave it a wave dispelling the vision.

"Do you understand now?"

Téa looked up at Leif, saw tears shining on his cheeks, heard them thick in his voice, just like his father. Or who they'd thought was his father. She wasn't quite sure what Vainquir was trying to tell them.

"I understand that my mom and dad were in your stupid Moon cult," said Leif.

Vainquir looked mildly amused. "Indeed, they were."

Leif trembled, let go of Téa's hand to scrub at his face. She wanted to scream at the old man in front of them. Didn't he care that he'd hurt someone? Didn't he see Leif's pain? Even as she didn't understand why she cared so much, her heart ached for Leif.

He reminds me of your father. Darla's words came to her in the near silence. The only sound was Leif's crying. Darla had meant Leif. And her father was blond, just like Leif was. "Oh!"

Vainquir looked at her, smiled knowingly, infuriatingly. Leif didn't seem to hear her.

"You see it now, don't you?"

"I, I think so," she answered. So, Leif had been born in the cult, and Charles wasn't his father; that much seemed clear. Was it Terry? Or was it someone else?

"Unions must only be between the committed ones, unless they first make arrangements with me. The ones that gave life to both of you never asked for this permission." Vainquir looked first at Leif. "Your identity was a secret until She-that-has-no-name came along. Then the Moon revealed all to me."

Vainquir sounded like a nut-job which made Téa feel a little braver. She stepped away from Leif. "Okay, so let's see if what I think *is* correct. You thought that Leif was the son of Charles and Elaine, but really he was the son of Elaine and someone else, not Charles."

Vainquir nodded.

"And then," began Téa. A sudden rush of adrenalin coursed through her as the reality hit her hard. She dropped to the ground. "Oh my god! My mother . . . my mother is Elaine Noble too?"

"She is."

She pointed in the direction where the images had appeared. "She was carrying me. I was She-that-has-no-name."

Téa received a nod from the old man.

Both joy and dismay filled Téa. This explained so much. The anger, the fighting. Why would any woman want to raise a kid that wasn't her own? But why didn't her real mother want to keep her? So many other questions, like why she was called She-that-has-no-name instead of a cult name. And who was the other pregnant woman?

Another adrenalin shot. Was it Gate's mother? Her own tears blurred her vision. She wrapped her arms around herself, sobbing and trying to understand. From somewhere far away, she could hear Leif speaking, but she couldn't comprehend the meaning.

Leif's world was crumbling. His mother was also Téa's mother. Her father was his father. That's why Elaine was always so stiff and controlled. She'd had an affair. Not once, but twice. Or had it been one long love fest?

What did that mean for his life now? Was he going to have to tell his parents, Téa's parents, that they knew all their dirty secrets? Was Jeremy even his brother?

"What about Jeremy?" he shouted at Vainquir. "Whose kid is he really, huh? Did you make them do this? Did they have any choice? Maybe the stupid moon told *them* something too!"

"Thoth, you must calm down."

"Don't call me that!" Leif screamed at the old man so hard his chest hurt. "My name is Leif!" Then suddenly Téa was there, her eyes red, her cheeks wet. Standing next to him, she addressed Vainquir.

"Do you know all about Gate too? That's who the others were. His parents. Isn't that right? Is he Elaine's kid too? What kind of messed up Moon cult was it? Why did my mother give me away? Why didn't I get--"

"Téa," shouted Vainquir, "you must calm down. All your answers will come in time."

She and Leif both took a deep breath as if their breathing was in sync. The smirk on the old man's face didn't go unnoticed. Leif gave Téa's shoulder a squeeze, hoping she understood, hoping she saw it too.

"She didn't give you away, dear child," said Vainquir after a moment's pause. "She only sent you to live with your father. It was the arrangement they came up with on their own."

"Why didn't Elaine and Terry stay together then, if we were their kids?" asked Téa.

"Yeah," agreed Leif. "Wouldn't that have made more sense? Then we wouldn't be here needing to fix it!"

Vainquir smiled like he knew something Leif and Téa didn't. Leif realized the old man probably knew a whole lot they didn't want to know. His mind whirled. It seemed simple to him. But this was a cult his (their) parents had gotten involved with. Everything they did probably had deep roots. Vainquir spoke again, this time addressing Téa. "Because you were unborn, you knew no parents. Leif only knew one father, so they decided that Koon and Myst remain together. It was only fair, really. And Erla accepted you for the sake of your father. She loves you."

Téa shook her head. "No, she loves *him*. Enough to raise his bastard daughter."

"Who decided?" asked Leif. "You or them. And what about Jeremy?"

Vainquir looked at him, giving Leif the creeps, but he held the old man's gaze. "I did not force them. They chose to *break* my rules of their own accord, and they chose their own path."

Obviously, he didn't know anything about Jeremy. That had to mean that Jeremy was born after they'd left the cult, or had been kicked out, and that he was truly Charles's son.

"She-that-has-no-name," he bellowed, even though there was no reason to raise his voice. "There is one more thing. Your parents have another secret, and still do not know how I discovered it."

They stood there in the semi-darkness, lit only by the moon and Vainquir's staff. When he didn't speak, Téa asked, "Well, what else did they do?"

"They were young at the time and so your grandparents raised her."

So cryptic. Leif wondered if Téa knew what Vainquir was talking about, and got his answer when she replied, "I don't understand."

Suddenly it was clear to Leif. When he'd seen her parents in the basement, her mother had been pregnant, and Téa said Erla didn't have her in high school. "Téa, you have an older sibling. I mean, not me but someone else. Remember I saw your mom in the school basement? The baby they sacrificed?"

Leif could almost see the wheels turning in Téa's brain as she considered his question. He turned to glance at Vainquir, who stood there grinning like an idiot, waiting for them to put it all together. Leif wanted to reach out and punch him.

"Had Myst and Nylo not had their little fling, Morgana and Nylo would have been cast out anyway for keeping her a secret from me.

Secrets are not to be kept from the Moon family. And they did not sacrifice her."

With that, Vainquir was gone. The moon brightened in his absence and the images of war were back though somewhat faded. Diamonds sparkled on the Commerce as it flowed past, far below them. A white ceramic table had appeared in the middle of the field. On it sat a plate with what appeared to be two Joe Louis cakes, except instead of chocolate, the coating was red velvet.

"What are those for?" asked Leif.

"Huh?" Téa glanced briefly in the direction he was pointing, her mind still elsewhere. "I don't know. They're just Moon pies."

Moon pies. That made sense, but what were they here for?

"It's Darla," sang out Téa. "It has to be her."

"What? Who?"

"Darla. She must be the one he was talking about, the one he said was raised by my grandparents. She was raised as Mom's sister, my aunt. Mom would have been in high school when she was born. And that means, if Mom, I mean Erla and Dad had her, she's my, our, half sister. We all have the same father."

"Then that would make Jeremy my half-brother."

"*Our* half-brother," Téa corrected. "We have the same mother."

"Ewww," cried Leif, recalling how he'd urged Jeremy to date her. "You two didn't, you know, kiss or anything did you?"

Téa smacked him in the arm. "No, you idiot! We're just friends."

Leif scratched his head. "Okay, so Erla and Terry had Darla before they joined the cult. Then Terry and Elaine had me and you. Right so far?"

"From what I can tell, yes."

"Then they left, or got kicked out, and Elaine and Charles had Jeremy. Does that work out right?"

"My head hurts thinking about it, but yes. I'm pretty sure it does."

Satisfied that their assessments were correct, Leif remained silent, as did Téa. Tears had dried, but thoughts still ran rampant. At least Leif's did and he was sure his sister's did too. Sister. That had a strange ring to it.

"What if we did?" she said finally. "Me and Jeremy. What if we did get romantically involved? What would they have done, Leif? Would anyone have tried to stop us? Would they have told us the truth or just made up a bunch of excuses?"

Leif shuddered. Those were excellent questions. Questions which, he realized, he might never get answers to. Maybe he didn't even want any.

Chapter Twenty—Choices

"So, our parents broke the rules. They kept secrets and had affairs," mused Leif, as he stood in Demon's field, gazing toward the Commerce River. Thick fog blocked his view. "So why the marks?"

Téa didn't respond. She heard his question, but she hadn't quite worked that out yet. Her mind exploded with all the information she'd just been given. Not the least of which was Vainquir's name for her mother: Morgana. At first, she wasn't sure, but as she untangled facts and lies and made connections, it was the only thing that made sense. Myst was Elaine's cult name and Morgana was Erla's. That's why her father often referred to her as Morgan. Not *Captain* Morgan after all. And if Thoth was a Moon god's name, then maybe they all were.

"I can answer that." Sen's voice rang out in the silence.

Téa watched him cross the field through dense haze that reached for his knees. Scanning the area, she noted that everything was foggy now. White wispy threads wound through the forest and thicker ones obscured the image of the castle. Only the three of them were there.

"He brought us here," said Téa, pushing her focus elsewhere. "Vainquir drew us in with the blood and the visions. And we needed the marks for that, right?"

"Yes. The marks also allowed us to track you. You had to know the truth one day. Without knowing, there was no chance for the circle to be whole again. You also had to be old enough to understand what was happening to you."

"But why couldn't you just tell us?" asked Leif.

"If Vainquir had shown up at your door, an ancient, wizened man, would you have believed him? Supposing your parents would even let him in to speak with you. They knew the mark belonged to us, but they were unaware of what it really was. They only knew we had marked you."

"Okay," agreed Leif, "so we wouldn't have believed you. But why the visions, the blood and the whole deal at the school? Wasn't there any other way?"

"What would you suggest?" asked Sen, a glint in his eye, but whether sinister or simply amusement, Téa couldn't tell.

When Leif didn't respond, Sen went on. "The blood connected you to us. The visions connected you to each other, and the "deal at the school" not only caused you to trust and rely on each other, but also allowed you to come to your own conclusions. In your own time. No matter how long it took. You needed to reach the truth on your own."

"But we didn't reach the truth," argued Leif. "We suspected it had something to do with a cult, but Vainquir told us everything."

"You had to be open to the truth, to accept each other before learning who you really were. Without learning to work together, you never would have made it here to obtain the truth. Nor would you be able to make the choice you must now make."

"Choice?" asked Téa. "Are we sacrifices? Do we have to die or something?" She projected her voice with more bravado than she felt. What had their parents condemned them to?

Sen shook his head. "No. We do not require death sacrifices. You and your brother must only make one decision. Together. As you have been learning to do. Vainquir is pleased with the results you have shown. This will help with what you now must do."

Results? Like they were some kind of experiment? Leif said nothing, just crossed his arms, and looked at Sen as if cheat notes were written on the man's face.

Sen returned the gaze. Bulls staring one another down. Téa wouldn't have been surprised to see them go at one another. For what though? Was Sen reading Leif's mind? Was Leif looking for easy answers?

"Hey," she shouted at them, getting their attention. They both swung their heads toward her. "What about Gate Williams? His parents were there too, right?"

Sen grinned and his eyes glinted. Téa, suddenly afraid, backed up a step.

"His parents," said Sen in a slow, throaty voice, "did not break the rules."

A second, that seemed an eternity, later, Leif stepped between Téa and Sen, who hadn't taken his eyes off her. "What are we supposed to do now?"

"Choose." Sen returned his gaze to Leif. "You can choose to make the circle whole, or you can leave it broken." His eyes cut to Téa. "One of those choices will bring a better life, will put love right. I cannot tell you which."

"Then how are we supposed to choose?" growled Leif.

Téa's nails bit into her palms again. This time she flung her fingers open, stretching them, trying to break herself of that old habit.

"If I tell you, it's like cheating, giving you the answer to a test. And only one choice will keep the Motherhood of the Moon alive."

Then Sen was gone, the fog with him.

The morning dawned all over again. The sun shone bright and warm in the sky, but so did the moon. A small, unblemished orb diminished by sun sister. The gray castle glistened peacefully in the glow. But there was no sound, only an eerie silence.

"I think we should choose to fix the circle," Téa said softly. It seemed a no brainer to her. Repair what once went wrong and get a better life. Let Terry and Elaine be together, if that's how it was meant to be. Maybe then, she thought, there'd be no more screaming. Having Leif as a big brother didn't seem so bad in comparison.

"Why?" asked Leif. "What if I like my life the way it is? And what if that's the choice that saves the cult?"

"So? I want a better life. I hate the one I have now."

"What about me? I like mine perfectly fine. And what if our parents are still in the cult when we go back, and nothing has changed?"

"How can nothing change if we fix what's broken?" Téa stomped off, unaware that her hands were clenched. She plopped herself down to stare out at the Commerce River. Tears started to flow. She dropped her head to her knees.

A few minutes later, she sensed Leif sitting beside her, felt his hand gently caress her back. "I'm sorry you have a terrible life." He sighed. "Téa, are we even going to remember any of this? No matter what choice we make, what's going to happen when we go back? *If* we go back."

She wiped her eyes with the heels of her hands and lifted her head to meet his gaze. At the sight of her face, his expression saddened. Somehow, he cared for her. Somehow, she knew.

"We have to remember. It's who we are. And as long as we choose, we can go back. At least that was my understanding. We can't stay here forever, can we?"

"But what if choosing to leave the circle broken makes our lives better?"

"If the circle stays broken, you've changed nothing. How can that make our lives better?" A sob hitched in Téa's throat.

Leif's hand rose to her shoulders. "But aren't we changing things just by being here?"

"Then why would we have to make a choice?"

"Dammit, Téa, I don't know. But I know I don't want to give up what I have now." He pulled his hand away. "And I don't want our parents in some sort of cult. That means we would be too."

"Not necessarily. You said Atlas was there in the basement. Maybe *he* talked them all into joining the cult. If we make the right choice, maybe that won't happen."

"You don't know that. Maybe Atlas has nothing to do with anything."

"Leif, we don't know anything. What about the affair they had? Is that why your parents hired mine? Were they all involved in one big orgy?"

Leif looked surprised. As if that hadn't occurred to him. Could that be true? Why would her mother and Leif's father want to work with the people who'd betrayed them? Were they covering up, or was that some sort of cult punishment too?

A rumble echoed around them and, at first, Téa thought it was thunder. She glanced at the sky. Not a cloud anywhere.

"Téa, look!" He pointed toward the castle behind them.

Turning, she saw soldiers, wearing red coats and black and white Tricorn hats, falling from the castle to the ground.

Watching their descent, she saw that once they landed, they shouldered their muskets and shot at the Indigenous people who had reappeared. Behind them, the settlers scrambled about in chaos. The Natives gathered bows and arrows. She frowned and wondered what was happening now. "Your life might be fine, but--"

The rest of what she said was lost in more gunfire. She barely heard herself, so she knew Leif certainly hadn't. What did it matter anyway? He liked his perfect life.

"What about Jeremy and Darla? Whose kids will they be if we fix it? Or, if we don't?" he asked as the reverberation faded away, but only for a moment.

The scene beyond them grew more chaotic. People screamed and children cried. People, shot by bullets or arrows, dropped where they stood then disappeared as if they were in some ethereal video game.

Téa's hands clenched but she forced them open again, splaying her fingers. "Why can't they just live in peace?" She grabbed handfuls of her shirt, wringing the cloth, fingers aching.

Even amidst the chaos, she knew Leif had made a good point, or at least a thought-provoking one. Whose kids indeed? Darla had been born to Terry and Erla *before* they'd joined the cult, so that had to stay the same, didn't it? What about Jeremy? Vainquir didn't seem to know about him. Why couldn't Sen have told them more? It was like trying to order food without knowing what was on the menu.

Suddenly Leif's fingers were on her chin, turning her face to him. "Sin broke the circle, Téa. Betrayal. The same thing is happening here. Betrayal." He pointed to the chaos, then to the two of them. "Them, us. Once there is agreement, there is peace."

She looked into his eyes. "Well, duh. What are you trying to say? That I have to agree with you to stop this?"

A wind blew up, whipping their hair around their faces, carrying the screams to their ears. This was beginning to feel too much like home for Téa. She pulled away from Leif and started running down the hill, trying to leave the bloody scene behind.

Her newly discovered brother ran after her; she heard him call out to her, "No, wait!"

She kept running, then tripped on a stone embedded in the ground, and pitched forward. Momentum slid her a little farther, grass staining her hands. Then Leif was there, picking her up, the wind still furious around them. "No, Téa, *I'm* agreeing with *you*. We have to fix the circle."

"But what about your fancy life?" she sobbed, as he held her hands in his.

"I don't know. Maybe it'll still be that way. But you were right. It has to be fixed. Leaving it broken doesn't change things."

The screams and gunshots faded away along with the wind. Téa watched over Leif's shoulder and saw the scene shimmer away.

Indigenous people went about their daily chores in Demon's field. The castle was gone. Leif had made a good choice, she thought. Things had been put right.

Sen appeared again, no fog accompanying him this time. He carried a tray in his hands. Téa nodded in his direction and Leif turned. "What does he want *now*?" he groaned.

As Sen approached, Téa could see the red Moon pies from the table on the plate, along with a small knife. "One last thing," he announced. "Well, two really. Could you please hold this? In your right hand." He held the plate out to Téa then picked up the knife. "May I see your marks."

Leif snorted. "May I? You say that like we have a choice."

Sen remained silent, waiting. Leif offered his right arm first. Sen made a small incision. Then he did the same to Téa's left arm. "Now, with the blood running free, you shall eat the Moon cake."

Téa stifled a laugh. He said, "Moon cakes" as if they were some sort of magical food item. She recalled the lumpy mess in the sink in the basement. Had that been some kind of old cake? Did these red velvet Moon pies represent some sort of cult food? Were they imbued with perceived magic? Drugs?

With a quick glance at each other, they both took a cake. Téa studied it, hesitating. What would happen once they bit into it? After they ate the whole thing? Another glance at Leif for guidance. He inspected the cake as Sen patiently waited. Then with a look at Téa, and a shrug, he raised it to his mouth. She did the same. They bit into their cakes at the same time.

They tasted great, but as they chewed, Sen, the plate and the cakes disappeared.

Everything went dark first. Then the dark was replaced by bright white light, and stale, sterile air.

Chapter Twenty-One— Remembering

Leif pulled his shirt over his head. Stupid! He'd been so stupid! He paused with the shirt halfway on. Stupid? What had been stupid? Whatever thought had been in his head faded as though it had never been there.

"Leif, dear, are you okay?"

He jumped at the sound of her voice, then in one swift movement, pulled his shirt down over his body and turned. "Mom!"

Elaine smiled. "We had quite a scare, but everybody's fine." She frowned then, and her voice grew stern. "Next time wear your gear. I don't care if it *is* just a ride around the block."

Gear? Ride? What was she talking about. He held out his right arm, but instead of finding a tattoo, he found road rash along his forearm, and on his hand. He looked at the other arm and found the same.

"You're lucky that's all you got, just some scraping and bruising," his mom said. She didn't get to say anything further when a nurse poked her head in through the doorway.

"Everything is good, Dr. Noble. Everyone can leave now."

Dr. Noble! So, it *was* all a dream. But what had really happened? Where had the scrapes come from? Had Téa been with him? Why?

"Your father is with Téa, so let's go."

He followed his mother from the room, only to go into another room. Was she visiting a patient? Looking in on Téa?

A curtain hung across the room and Terry Smith stood there with his back to it. He smiled. "She's just changing back into her clothes."

My father? That's Téa's father. No, a voice whispered inside his head. He's your father too.

"How're you doing?" Terry asked.

"Ah, fine." But Leif didn't feel fine. His body was sore, and he was confused. Something had changed; Terry was his father now, but why?

"Are you sure?" asked Terry.

Leif shook his head. "I don't know. Something feels off."

"All his scans were normal," said Elaine, sounding worried.

"Can I talk to him alone?" asked Téa from behind the curtain. Leif heard her zip something up. Jeans? An overnight bag?

Elaine and Terry looked at each other, strange looks on their faces. "Are you sure?" asked Terry again.

"Yes."

"Okay, try not to kill one another," chuckled Elaine.

But it wasn't funny. Leif panicked. Is that what had happened, had they really tried to kill one another? No, of course not. His mother had said to wear his gear next time. An image of a motorbike flashed through his head. Did he have one? He realized his parents were looking at him. He nodded, hoping that was what they were expecting. Apparently, it was; they walked out of the room together.

Téa pushed the curtain open then sat on the bed. "Have a seat," she said, sweeping her hand in a gesture to include both the bed and a chair that sat under a window next to a locker.

Her arms also had road rash, as well as her left cheek. There was a stitched slash above her left eye. That's going to leave a scar, he thought, wondering if she was angry with him for blemishing her face. "What happened?" he asked, reaching up to touch his own face. Some road rash there too, but nothing else.

"You don't remember?"

Leif shook his head, then looked into her eyes. Amber, just like Jeremy's. Her hair brown, just like Jeremy's. Then the memories came flooding back. Vainquir and the school. The moon and the sin of their parents. The visions and the blood. Except in this reality, everything was different because he and Téa had changed things. In this reality he'd crashed his motorbike, and neither of them had been wearing helmets or any sort of gear. They were just going around the block. That's what had been so stupid. He remembered now. All of it, including the discarded beer bottle, the broken bottom half of a brown bottle lying on the side of the road right where they'd skidded and fallen. Her head had slammed against the sharp, jagged edge. Damned littering idiots.

He sat on the bed. "I'm so sorry. That guy came out of nowhere. But still, it was all my fault. I should have made sure we at least had helmets on." He looked at the gash again, wishing it was on his own face.

Téa put her hand on Leif's arm. "*We* should have made sure we were wearing helmets. I'm a big girl, you know." She smiled. "But it's okay. We're both here and alive. Do you remember Vainquir?"

"Yes, but like a dream or something. So, who are we now exactly? My mind's foggy on that."

"Not surprising, considering it took you so long to figure it out."

"So long? Can you blame me? What a mess that was!"

Téa grinned. "I'm kidding. But I *did* figure it out first." She stuck her tongue out at him.

Leif rolled his eyes. "Okay, whatever."

Téa grabbed her phone from where it lay on the hospital bed and began thumbing information into it. "I want to be able to remember this."

"So, you're typing the whole story down now?"

"No . . ." her voice trailed off as her thumbs worked furiously. Finally, she showed him the screen.

Vainquir = Moon Master

Elaine (Our Mom also Jeremy's mom) = Myst

Terry (Our Dad also Darla's dad) = Nylo

Erla (mother of Darla) = Morgana

Charles (father of Jeremy) = Koon

Leif = Thoth

Téa = She That Has No Name?

Sen = ?Minion?

"Does this information look correct to you? Terry and Elaine are our parents now, Charles is Jeremy's father, I think."

He held up his hand, quieting her, reading the screen. "I think so. Somehow it makes sense to me anyway. Wait, who's She-that-has-no-name?"

"Me. It says so right there."

"Yeah, but I don't remem––oh wait, yeah I do remember. That's what those two creepy guys called you."

"Yes."

Leif rubbed the rash on his face. "Okay, so Mom is still a doctor. What else?"

"Charles is too, near as I can tell. Dad is the manager at The Brick. But I don't remember where he worked before." She pocketed her phone. "Tell me something, Leif. How do you feel about only having one parent as a doctor? And one as just a store manager? You know you won't have as much money as you did with two doctor parents."

He considered that. Doctors made good money, but manager wages weren't anything to complain about. He had a bike in this reality, not a car. But what about . . . what? Examining his inner feelings, he found he was content. He hadn't lost everything and, he realized, Téa had gained so much more. Strangely, that made him happy. "Yeah, I'm good," he replied. "But what about your mom? I mean Erla."

"I'm not sure on that one. I think Darla lives with her though." She smiled. "I'm still a little foggy on some things too."

"You two almost done in there?" asked Terry. "The others are waiting downstairs for you."

"What others?" Leif lowered his voice to ask Téa.

She shrugged, then called out that they'd be out in a minute before answering her big brother. "Darla and Jeremy, maybe?"

"Vainquir didn't know about Jeremy, did he? Sen either."

"I don't think so. He must have been born after our parents left the cult."

After they left the cult. Was Charles really still Jeremy's father now? How could it be?

"Do you think it's still around?" Téa interrupted his thoughts.

"Probably. Somewhere anyway. What about Gate?"

"The orderlies are here," called out Elaine before Téa could respond.

"What for?" asked Leif.

Elaine came into the room followed by two men, neither of whom were Terry. Both of them had wheelchairs.

"But I can walk fine," protested Leif.

"Me too," added Téa. Then her eyes went wide.

One of the interns had long, red hair pulled back into a ponytail. Grey strands streaked through it. His wrinkled hands looked old, and his smile, that of a younger man, creeped her out. He had soft brown eyes, and a tattoo on his right cheek. A red circle slashed through with a solid jagged line. A smaller solid red circle lay to one side of it. Sen! Or was it Vainquir. A light scent of roasted chicken wafted through the air. If Leif noticed, he didn't react.

"Hi," said the other intern. He didn't have a tattoo. Not a visible one anyway. "My name is Sam, and this is Vance Menzie. You actually might have heard of him. He released a CD not too long ago. Chants. If you're into that."

Téa choked in surprise. Chants?! Now Leif did look at her. Sam mistook her reaction and went on. "I guess not, eh? But I'll bet you're anxious to get out of here."

"More than you know," said Téa and sat herself in the wheelchair he offered.

Leif reluctantly sat in Vance's chair. Whether it was because he recognized the man or he just didn't want a wheelchair ride, Téa had no idea, and no intention of asking about it.

When they got to the bottom floor, they found that the others were Jeremy, Darla, Gate, and Kim. As soon as Téa saw them, all her new memories came flooding back. Darla was her half-sister. They shared a father--Terry. He and Erla had dated in high school, and Darla had been born a few months after they'd graduated. Shortly after that they broke up. Now Darla lived with her mother and stepfather on the other side of the Commerce where Erla was a secretary for a law firm. Had they ever been a part of the cult in this new restored reality?

Then there was Jeremy. Jeremy! He was her twin brother now. The three of them were all Terry and Elaine's kids. She'd have to remember to change that in her notes.

She squeezed her fingers together in her lap, trying not to appear as overwhelmed as she was. As far as her family knew, she'd only come in overnight for tests after the bike accident, and not wearing a helmet. Mild concussion was all she had in addition to a laceration that was sure to scar. It didn't matter, though; she could always cover it with makeup if it bothered her too much. She was lucky. Who, or what, she wondered, was responsible for her, for them, not getting any worse injuries.

Kim rushed over to Leif, gushing about how worried she'd been.

Téa managed a smile as Gate, with his goofy grin, came over to help her up. She almost told him no, that she could do it herself. But he knew that, she realized. He just wanted to help; he was her boyfriend. Kim was Leif's girlfriend. Téa wondered what other surprises were in store.

Epilogue

Téa gets off the bus and looks around for Gate. He's nowhere in sight. Does she have enough time to run across the street for a coffee? Just as she pulls her phone out of her kangaroo pocket, a text notification dings. Gate!

Meet me in caf by popmachn

Shoving the phone back into the pocket, she enters the school and heads to the cafeteria. The clatter of pans and dishes meets her as she approaches her destination, cafeteria workers already getting things ready for the lunch crowd.

But no Gate.

She glances at the clock above the pop machine just inside the cafeteria kitchen. Even over the sounds of food prep, she hears its ticking.

"Gate, where are you?" she mutters. "Classes are going to start soon."

"Boo!"

She jumps as he grabs her from behind, then extends one hand out in front of her. "Put this on."

"What is it?" A piece of black cloth lies draped over his palm.

"A blindfold."

"What for?" She turns to face him. "Gate, classes will be starting soon, and I still need to go to my locker."

"We have time." He points to a pile of books on a table in the cafeteria. "Our books are right there. I've got yours all ready."

"Oh." They'd exchanged locker combinations, but now a small voice in the back of her mind tries to raise a red flag. It's only Gate, she thinks, ignoring it and giving in to his request. Gate ties the blindfold behind her head. "Can you see?"

She pushes a bit of cloth up and peeks beneath it. "I can now."

He swats at her hand. "But you can't see with it on?"

"No."

She hears the faint thud of his fingertips on the table as he grabs the books, then guides her, calling out where to turn and where there are steps. Voices, the hum of computers, and the ring of a phone alert her to their location. He keeps going, onto the ramps for the disabled students on the bottom floor. But why?

"Gate," she says peeking again.

He's leading her toward the elevator next to a washroom.

"What?" he asks, turning toward her. Seeing her lifting the cloth, he says, "I told you not to peek."

"This is stupid!"

"No, it isn't."

She drops the cloth with another sigh and lets him take her on the elevator. Why on earth are they going down to the basement? There's nothing down there but a shop class and garage, a few storage rooms, the janitor's office, and a couple of washrooms. What can he possibly want to show her down there?

Finally, they stop. Though there's no sound except the hum of an elevator and Atlas whistling, she's certain there's someone else here. Watching them. A chill runs down her spine, and she reaches for the blindfold in near panic. "Gate! Can I take it off *now*?"

"You can. Let me untie it."

She doesn't wait for that. She rips it off and finds Jeremy, Leif and Kim standing outside Atlas's office, each holding a balloon and grinning.

Gate leans in, as if for a kiss, but instead whispers in her ear, "I know what really happened." Then he pulls away. She frowns at him. What is he talking about? She looks at the others.

"Gate arranged this," says Kim, the hand not holding the balloon hanging onto Leif's.

Leif rolls his eyes. "He seemed to think you deserved a big party after one night in the hospital."

"Hey, she's my special girl and her dumbass brother let her get hurt." He gently fingers the bandage over her left eye.

Then it's Téa's turn to roll her eyes. But she also smiles at Gate. He's a great boyfriend, but sometimes he can be silly.

"There's more," Gate says. "Or at least there will be."

She groans and shakes her head. "I wasn't gone that long."

Then a woman steps from inside the office. At first Téa doesn't recognize her. She has short black hair, one lock of which is pure white. Diana! An image of a figure in a robe explodes in Téa's mind. She presses her hand to her forehead.

"Oh my gosh, Téa, are you okay?" asks the woman who Téa suddenly remembers is Gate's mother, Cassie. She and Erla, no, Elaine were pregnant at the same time, just before Elaine and Terry were banished, along with Erla for keeping Darla a secret.

"Did you just call my mom Diana?" Gate has a horrified look on his face.

Téa doesn't realize she'd said that out loud. Who is Diana?

"No, I don't think so. I don't know." She presses her fingers to her temple. Her head has begun to ache.

Leif pulls away from Kim and puts a hand on Téa's shoulder. "Maybe you're not ready to be back here. Do you want to go home?"

"Oh no," cries Cassie. "Gate wanted to have a special party for you. Atlas let me use his office, and after school I'm going to bring cake for everyone."

In the seconds between when she stops talking and Gate starts, Téa hears Atlas humming. Or maybe he's chanting.

"Anything for my girl," Gate says.

Then the warning bell rings. Five minutes to get to class.

"Let's meet back here after school," Gate tells them. "We can have cake, and I'll run over to Tim's for coffees."

"Look," says Leif. "This is too much for her right now. Gate, I'll call you later. Or she will." He takes Téa's arm and leads her back down the hall.

There's a buzz as the others talk among themselves. Or are they all chanting? Téa checks her arm.

"It's not there," says Leif.

She doesn't respond, nor does she speak as Leif leads her out to his car. Once inside, he pounds the steering wheel with his fist. "Damn! I thought we weren't supposed to remember any of that stuff?"

"Did anyone actually say that?" She recalls Gate's words and ice forms in her gut.

"I don't know, Téa, but it obviously has had an effect on you."

She lays her head back against the seat and sighs. "I just got a flash of a person in a robe, and the name Diana with it. I don't even know anyone named Diana. And Gate just told me *he* knows what really happened."

"What?" Leif yells, twisting to face her.

"Yeah." Pulling out her phone, she taps the screen to bring up the notes she'd made earlier and shows them to Leif again.

Vainquir = Moon Master = Vance Menzies?

Elaine (Mom) = Myst

Terry (Dad also Darla's dad) = Nylo

Erla (mother of Darla) = Morgana

Charles (father of Jeremy) = Koon

Leif = Thoth

Téa = She That Has No Name

Sen = ?Minion?

"Oh yeah, we got this one wrong." She points to where it says Charles (father of Jeremy) = Koon. "I forgot to change it."

She changes it so it reads:

Charles = Koon (father to Jeremy in alternate reality)

Jeremy = Son of Terry and Elaine, twin to Téa, unknown in alternate reality

Then she spreads her fingers so that her pointer is on the first name, and her pinky, the last. "These guys were in the hospital, I'm sure of it."

"The orderlies."

Téa nods. "At least one of them was. I'm still not sure if they were both cult members, or only one. I'm pretty sure Vance was Vainquir."

"Okay, but what about Gate? How much does he actually know?" demands Leif.

"He didn't say. Look, it's like there's broken glass inside my mind, and I have to put it all back together." She sighs again. "But what if the cult *is* still here? And what if Gate is in it? You started to ask me about him in the hospital."

"I did?"

"Yes. You don't remember?"

"No."

"Oh."

"But I don't think our parents are in it this time around. Or still. Or whatever."

"No, but what if––" Téa thumbs more info into her phone, adding two more names to the list.

Cassie (mother of Gate) = ?Diana?

Gate = ??

"Does it matter? Téa, do *you* think the cult is still around and that the Williamses are in it?"

The red flag voice in her head tries to speak again, and once more she ignores it, and Leif's question. "Did you hear Atlas humming? While we were down in the basement a few minutes ago."

"Yeah, I guess."

"Humming or chanting?"

"Why?" Frustration in his voice. "Do you want me to take you home?"

She turns to face him, her own frustration mounting. "No. Why does Gate want to have a damn party for me, Leif? Why the stupid charade of going down to the basement? Why not just ask me to come over for cake after school?" Her voice rises with each sentence as ideas pour into her head. She feels both as if she knew this all along, and yet at the same time is just adlibbing. "Why can't we just go to his house?"

"Téa!" Leif reaches out and pulls her to him. Tears have begun to leak from her eyes.

"I can't do it, Leif. If Gate and his parents *are* in this cult, I can't. I just can't."

"I won't let anyone hurt you."

Her phone vibrates then and chimes with her chosen text tone. She pulls away to look at it. Gate. Her blood runs cold when she reads the message.

Hey you! I'd like to tlk 2 u about this creed my parents have. c u after school she-that-has-no-name Oh, and don't forget to bring Thoth.

# # #

Atlas sits on a chair in the corner of his office, doing something on his phone. Which seems strange since Jeremy has never seen him with a phone.

Cassie (Diana?) busies herself with preparations. Gate's father, Roman, a slim man with thick silvery-grey hair pulled into a ponytail, had called her both. Maybe Téa was right. Maybe it is too much. Jeremy's insides squirm as if he's having a panic attack even though he never has before. He's channelling Téa's feelings. It's happened before, but since she was in that coma, it happens a lot more often. Sometimes he gets dream-flashes of things that don't make sense, like talking to her and Leif on a TV screen or seeing his face inside a moon. Sometimes Téa is standing in a bright shaft of moonlight with a red-haired man.

Welcome back Téa!

The words, written in red gel on top of white frosting, are on a slab cake sitting on Atlas's desk. Such writing reminds Jeremy of some of the old books that Téa is fond of. Is that why Gate had asked for it that way? Who had he even gotten to do it? Roman Williams runs a delicate finger around the bottom of the cake, gathering icing. There's a small bandage on his neck, a bit of red peeking out beneath it. Blood or a tattoo? wonders Jeremy. A chill wanders down his spine, but he doesn't understand why.

"Roman!" reprimands his wife, as she sets out candles. The candles are red and white striped and have words carved into them, but Jeremy can't read what it says. Not without a closer look.

"She's coming, right?" asks Gate, his voice tight with worry.

Jeremy shrugs. "I guess."

"She's your twin sister," says Gate, as if that means Jeremy should know.

"That doesn't mean I know everything she will or won't do."

Gate checks his phone, then asks another strange question. "She has a half-sister too, right? Hidden Child. She lives with her mom."

Jeremy stares at him. Hidden Child? He's about to ask Gate, only half jokingly, what he'd smoked before coming here, but Cassie-Diana clears her throat and shoots Gate a look. Obviously, Téa had told him about Darla, but she was *their* half-sister, clearly not just Téa's.

"Well, I'm sorry," Gate shouts back, even though there was no reason to raise his voice. He seems frustrated and shakes his head. "Forget it. I'm not doing this."

"Oh, but you are, Gate," returns his mother. It almost sounds like a threat.

"Then you better remind Dad too. Diana!" Gate puts emphasis on the name. "Téa probably knew about it because she heard him calling you that."

What is going on? wonders Jeremy. Was that why Téa had called her Diana? She probably just thought it was Gate's mother's name, as he had. But was Roman even here this morning when Téa was? He can't remember. And so, who was Cassie?

A weird feeling starts gnawing at his gut. What kind of party had Gate arranged anyway? Because Jeremy's getting the feeling that it's more than just a welcome, and that he really shouldn't be here right now, or at all.

Gate's mother turns to his father and glares. Roman raises his hands in surrender and mumbles, "Yes, *Cassie*."

"Roger," she then snaps to Atlas. "Do you have them?"

Atlas nods and pats the locker beside him. "It's all in here."

Cassie nods in approval.

Jeremy's head swims. She's Cassie now? What does Atlas have? Just then Jeremy's phone beeps a text notification. He checks it out. It's Leif.

If yur wth gate, get away from him. Don't go 2 the party. Teas not going. Get away and call me

Jeremy puts his phone away and tries to think of an excuse to leave. He notices Gate texting on his phone. Then Gate looks up, a mix of fear, confusion and disappointment on his face. Maybe even a bit of anger sparking in his eyes. Cassie notices as well. "Gate?"

"Mom, Téa just texted me. She's not coming." He shoots a look at Jeremy, but Jeremy can't read it.

"What? Are you kidding me?" Her voice is on the verge of a screech and her cheeks redden.

Gate shakes his head and, as he engages in an argument with his mother, Jeremy slips away. A glance back reveals that Roman has noticed and is watching him. Jeremy ignores him and presses the elevator button. He pulls his phone out to call Leif.

"What's going on?" he asks when Leif picks up.

"I think the Williamses are dangerous. We need to talk."

Another chill runs down Jeremy's spine. Dangerous? The Williamses? He recalls the candles and the fancy script on the cake.

And what did Atlas have in that locker? He'll never get an answer to that, but he probably doesn't want one.

An image flashes in his mind, but too fast for him to catch what it is.

The Moon, Jeremy.

He spins around. There's no one there. The elevator doors open, and he steps out.

"What did you say?" he says into his phone.

"I said, meet us at Tim's. I'm with Téa."

"No, I mean about the moon."

"Jeremy," says Leif, his voice low and concerned. "I didn't say anything about the moon. Get over here now."

Jeremy hangs up.

Heading outside, he gets another text notification. This time it's Gate.

Hey Jeremy sory 4 what happend can u come back? Theres this creed my parents have and id like to tell u abot it.

The End

www.ingramcontent.com/pod-product-compliance
Lightning Source LLC
Chambersburg PA
CBHW070722010826
48977CB00006B/387